# The Backsliders

## Talia Scott

Copyright © 2024 Talia Scott

**All rights reserved.**

# Table of contents

Authors Foreword     4

I   prologue     5

II   Here comes sunday     11

III Heidi     22

IV Velma     29

V John Ferarri     35

VI That strange white boy
43

**VII Sugar rays**
51

**VIII Family business**
67

**IX Conference Day** 70

**X The backsliders** 86

**XI Family matters** 97

**XII epilogue**
109

## Author's Foreword

Before you move your fingers to read another word, I just want to send my appreciation to anybody who decides that my work is worthy enough to be consumed. This book is truly dear to my heart, it is not the ordinary faith based manuscript. One day I was sitting in my dorm room at my college campus and I started writing random scenarios about preacher kids who coincidentally lived in the 60s and eventually it turned into a story. I hope it doesn't come across as ordinary or cliche. So I want you to relax while you are reading and imagine for once that you are 10 or 11 or however old you were and you are at your favorite relatives house, spending the summer with your cousins and doing anything you guys may have been big and bad enough to do. Do you remember your grandmother frying chicken on the stove just before dinner was getting served? Are you that child that over heard about the church's board meetings even though it wasn't your business. Can you reminisce about a cold sip of lemonade on a scolding summer day and dreading the street lights coming on because it meant you had to go back inside. If you miss and recall the songs of old, and the deacons humming and opening up the church, and choirs wearing robes. This book may be for you. I hope readers can feel the love and passion that goes behind this. I want to thank every last one of my siblings MJ, Tanesha, Ben, Shakirah, Moriah and Madelyn, Sean, Bryson, Savannah And Eden. The Scott tribe for being a part of my inspiration and breathing life to these characters. And Thank my parents Marcus and Letisha for showing the love of God to me. The push was necessary to tell this story. I dedicate this story to every pastor's, preacher's kid who ever lived. And hopefully this time you can believe you have a voice in your world and also believe you matter. As my Bishop Michael A Blue quotes often, I pray that this book, although secular in its approach, will bring "pleasure to Christ's heart and fame to his name."

~

*Talia A. Scott*

## Chapter 1

*summer 1958*

*"years I spent in vanity*

*and pride caring not my lord was crucified*

*knowing it was not for me*

*he died on Calvary*

*mercy there was great and grace was free pardon there was multiplied to me*

*there my burdened soul found liberty*

*at the cavalry..."*

A great man once said that "a life spent making mistakes is not only more honorable, but more useful than a life spent doing nothing."This is agreeable but certain people will never understand the meaning. There's nothing like being a preacher's kid and having the pressure of people trying to tell you how to live your life.

And in a small town like Beverdille, The waters had all eyes on them. Along with their conscious and immense pressure to appease their folks. It was Sunday morning and David woke up to the smell of frying chicken and over in the next room, butterscotch perfume. The record that played a solemn tune in the parlor made its way up to David's bedroom. It dawned on him that it was probably communion Sunday, his mom picked out a black suit for him with a white collared shirt and pinstripe black, white and silver tie. They were in it for the long haul but that also meant dinner would be amazing. saints would show up on their doorsteps every sunday afternoon with dishes. That was the good part about church to David, the fellowship.

David quickly sprung out of bed and went to go to the bathroom, unfortunately somebody had beaten him to the punch.

"Heidi come on now hurry up, you know I gotta wash up." he commented aggressively banging on the bathroom door. Heidi unlocked the door and opened it just a little to take a peek at David with a smirk on her face he knew she wasn't gonna make this easy for him.

"Maybe you should have gotten your tail up when Mama waters said we're getting ready for church,"Heidi sassed. She then shut the door on him and went back to brushing her teeth. "Yeah keep brushing your teeth, no wonder we smell your hot breath in the car every Sunday." He retorted. He went on to the next bathroom but that seemed to be occupied too.
"Velma!". He chanted.

"David I'm bathing, go away." His slightly older sister ordered. "Man this ain't it." smacking his teeth, David went back to his room slamming the door shut.

You could hear both Heidi and Velma giggling in sync from each side of the hall. It was as if they planned it. That was further from the truth though. Mama waters always made an effort to wake the girls up earlier than David and his uncle. Because she would always say "ladies have many more things to take care of than you boys. The pretty boys can wait." She would joke.

At last mama waters was done with frying chicken and started preparing a sandwich for the reverend.

"Fried chicken..." comments Julius "the number one cause of high blood pressure for Americans." Julius was Reverend Water's baby brother. So little he was almost the kids' age. He had only turned 30,

While the other kids were either in high school or college. Julius was very educated but it served him no purpose. He fought in the Korean War a couple years back and had to move in with the waters. He felt like a burden but they were more than happy to have him. Because he was family and there was nothing like family.

"Boy hush let Ethel fix you something. That ain't no fact. Never read it in the health section of a newspaper."

Reverend Waters said, taking a large bite out of his crispy chicken leg. Julius sat back in the chair just chuckling.

"Where's the crew?" He questioned.

Ethel took notice and placed her fork on the table. "I don't know where they are." She says. "But they better hurry up if they don't want to miss breakfast before church." She yelled the last part so that they could hear upstairs. Only in the south

would it be normal to have a chicken dinner for breakfast as if they wouldn't revisit the food later.
It wasn't long before Heidi, Velma and David rushed down stairs.
Reverend Waters had gone through his pieces of chicken and Julius was pretty much full.
"There's only three pieces left?" David questioned.
"Yep." His mother answered shortly.
"Set an alarm clock next time" reverend waters demanded before taking a sip out of
His glass.
As you can see, family time was very important to
The waters. It came before just about anything. Except God. That was a revered belief system. He always taught his children and told them that there were three priorities in life and that was God,
Family and education. Anything else was just a liability.
Reverend Waters went into his study to button up his black collared dress shirt. He also grabbed his bible and journal and his ball point pin. He never went anywhere without his bible but even if he did leave it he already knew everything in it. And he didn't go to seminary school either.
"I was called by the lord, to cry loud and spare not." He would say. He would never knock those who were educated though. The truth was if he had the money back then to pursue school he would have done it. But life has a way of interrupting plans.

He met Ethel and they soon got married and started a life right away. Ethel was from north Hampton county from a very distinguished family and lived a privilege life as a negro girl. Her family even lived in France and Texas a few years before

coming back to North Carolina. While that was true, Ethel never forgot her southern roots; she only went out of the country for education but transferring back to America made no difference. You could be in the upper Ashland of society and no one would care because you're still just black .' And in Ethel's case her skin tone and family background got her through, yet she remained humble. She eventually met David sr. He worked for a textile company. He was not some insanely handsome model,other girls would fawn over.
He was rough around the edges, and a tall , noticeable man with warm chestnut coated skin. Ethel could see that he was sweet, considerate, and he loved God. Ethel loved him very much, she always had people in her family who said he wasn't good enough for her. That all changed when he became a minister.

In the parking lot of the Waters home there were three vehicles. All fords which was pretty affordable but still it was rare to see people in the negro community to own cars. Most folks rode on buses. And increasingly so because of the desegregation law that had just passed.
2 of the cars belonged to the reverend and the other car belonged to Julius. Julius was a mechanic, barber. Anything you needed him to be. The man was a jack of all trades. He even played the piano at church. And for that very reason he always had money.
"Hey! Why are you not coming?" David asked. "I'll be there before the sermon starts, Nephew." A smile crept up on David's face. He knew what his uncle was up to. Or it wasn't what he was up to but who he was into. "Nephew, you know they hold

service too long and just drag it for no absolute reason."Julius tilted his fedora and started driving out of the parking lot.

By this time everyone had made it to the family car. Everyone except Velma Waters'. "Always taking her precious time." Heidi commented, rolling her eyes. Ethel turned around and gave her a scornful look. "If you took your time you wouldn't look like a wild child all the time."

This was nothing new to Heidi. She loved her aunt but they had opposing views on womanhood. Heidi was a little too eccentric for Ethel's taste. David overheard his mothers comment and laughed right away. "Shut up David, I saw you coming in late last night." She whispered to him in a threatening tone.

Widening his eyelids,David pleaded with her to be quiet. Black mail was easily becoming a form of communication with the Waters kids.

"Okay guys I'm ready." Velma announced quickly grabbing the car door.

"Finally." The Reverend rejoices.

The Sunday adventure would begin.

## Chapter 2

'Here comes Sunday '

After a long but inspiring message the reverend stepped down from the pulpit and sat in his chair. It was almost set up like a throne. The head usher went to serve him a glass of apple juice while he summoned the assistant minister to give closing remarks and prayer. But everyone knew in the church that minister vixen was long winded. He didn't care if people wanted to go home and eat chicken. He'd make them feel guilty by saying "you think Moses or any of the prophets in the Bible were worried about a piece of chicken?" The answer was usually no. But David would murmur under his breath 'Moses had poor speech and he wasn't as long winded as you.' Luckily nobody could hear him say that while he was in the music department.

The choir stood up to sing. And David stood behind the organ to direct. The song was supposed to be sung by Aretha this Sunday but she had got caught up in other affairs and Reverend CL Franklin didn't bother to budge her. David's eyes moved toward the back where he saw the beautiful chocolate sister Loraine vixen. He mouthed " sing precious lord Rainy."
She looked at him with big eyes and a timid gaze.
"Are you crazy?" She whispers back. The still silence and private conversation back and forth had the congregation wondering. Lorraine felt pressure and soon started heading towards the stage from the choir stand. 'Praise the lord everybody.' She exclaimed now holding the mic that her father passed to her. "We're gonna sing a song that the Church Of

Christ temple deeply loves, precious lord." She completes giving a domineering smile.

"Well take your time honey." First Lady Waters says and then winks. Doing anything in front of a big congregation like that could be nerve wrecking. Rainy didn't see how the waters did it every Sunday and every bible study night on Wednesday's. She didn't know why David had put so much faith in her.

"Precious lord take my hand lead me on and let me stand. I am tired, I am weak and I am worn. Through the storm and through the night lead me on to the light." She coaxed. Rainy had a voice that could capture the ear of a drunk man out on the street. Her singing was soulful yet sweet. Some folks in the country thought she may have been the second coming of Mahalia Jackson and even compared her the newly debuted miss Franklin. But that wasn't the only thing David Jr. was thinking about.

When service came to an end, everyone migrated towards the front of the building. Leaving the deacon and the secretary sister Gracie to lock the church doors. Everyone stood on the grass conversing while reverend Waters tried to prepare himself to get back home. Not David though he had his eye on Lorraine and was currently stalling. He wishes he had the courage to make his move already.

Loraine, Heidi and Velma stood on the church steps giggling. Velma held her bible to her chest and tried balancing her huge decorative purse. Not to mention she wore stilettos, how did she keep her balance? Nobody knows. Heidi wore a big hat and an oversized dress with tan flats. Her style was very different compared to everyone else's but she was comfortable in her own skin. And Loraine dressed so classy almost similar to

Velma except she added her own twist in it. These three girls grew up together in the small town and were the best of friends. Eventually gaining some confidence, David glides to the girl's direction.
"Mmm mmm Miss Rainy.." David mutters.

"You sang that song today! You made me happy girl."
"Thanks minister David." Loraine shyly smiled. David chuckled at her shyness and thought it was funny that she called him minister. He was one but no young person ever thought to call him that.
Heidi smacks her teeth and grabs Lorraine by the arm. "Girl he ain't nobody. Let's go before Mama Water's leave."

"Okay." She answers begrudgingly. Her heart was beating fast and her mind didn't really move with her body. She glanced at David another time before being pulled off by the Water's girls.

Just before David could utter another word he felt somebody rubbing his head and ruffling his shoulders. "Hey pimp!!" "Jimmy?!" He exclaimed with excitement.
"In the flesh." James Howard was his name. He was about 5"10 and had caramel to pecan brown skin. His hair slicked back to look like smokey Robinson or something. He even had one gold tooth.
'A good for nothing thug is what he is' David was so used to hearing his big sister Velma say.
"Where were you today?" David asked. It was the same old same thing with little Jimmy. He got invited to church every-time he came around the waters. But did he ever really go? 'No.'

"Well you see I worked late last night man and by the time I got up y'all was probably in that long testimony service." He voiced
"Sure you're right." David answered his best friend skeptically. He knew little Jimmy wasn't really thrilled about church like that. And that was perfectly fine but one way or another he was gonna convince him to come back.
"How is it... you're always late for church but you're able to be at the dinner table before I get there?" David Joked. Jimmy just shook his head.
"Come on men, let's get to the house. I want some of your mama's peach cobbler." Jimmy mentioned.
Few tried but no one ever came close to the first lady's peach cobbler.

While everyone else was still talking on the church lawn. Ethel grabbed the girls and drove back to the house. She had no time to waste if she was going to be preparing a big dinner for the saints. Deacon and his wife were coming. Assistant minister vixen and his family were coming and not to mention any uninvited guest. When the girls got to the house they ran up the stairs like a bunch of 8 year olds despite the fact they were in their teens and early 20s.
Velma went to the main bathroom to freshen up and Heidi and Lorraine went to Velma's room to sit on the bed. Lorraine kicked off her heels propping herself up on her elbow. Heidi threw her hat on the ground and moved to sit on the floor

"So what's up with you girl?" Rainy asked, looking at Heidi.
"Whatcha mean? Ain't nothing going on around here."

"Oh please, you're in college. You and Velma, I bet exciting things happen to y'all often."
"Yeah but forget college. It's summer break now." Heidi whined.
"Nope you owe me details." Lorraine told her mischievously. You see Lorraine vixen was 19 but she never went to college because her parents couldn't afford it and partly because they wanted her to stay around home to help with church affairs.
"College is a great educational experience but it's just another 4 year school. The boys are cute but they're dumb." Heidi explained, rolling her eyes. Heidi was 20 years old. She was convinced that she may never find love and or never get married. The guys in the south just weren't her preference. Everything was so chauvinist in the south and the women hardly had a say in anything in her perspective.

"They just aren't mature enough for me." Velma heard their conversation while walking in with a towel wrapped around her. "Well miss things, I happen to think the men at A&T are more than fine. You're just weird." She argued. Velma grabbed her under clothes and took out her pleated yellow pants and white bowed blouse. She went to the closest to pull out her white sneakers.

"Velma just because I want a guy to like something about me other than my hair and shape doesn't make me weird. " Heidi argues back.
"Are you trying to insult me? I like to dress nice it's
For me. Okay? And if a man notices that's just a plus." Velma had just buttoned up her pants and made direct eye contact with her sister. You'd never think that these two were really close

They way they'd argue. But it was really all love. There were clear differences between the two and they just needed to understand one another.

"And that's that." Lorraine butts in.

Both Velma and Heidi gave her a bewildered look and she looked back at them.

"What?!" "Nothing. Let's go downstairs y'all. I think I heard mama call us down." Velma said, finally tying up her blouse. They ran back down stairs and went to the kitchen. When they arrived Ethel was placing her tub of fried chicken on the foyer and then she started preparing the crust for her peach cobbler. Velma cautiously walked by her mother for she knew how Ethel felt about wearing pants. Especially on a Sunday. She said it wasn't lady-like and that frustrated the heck out of her.

"People will be coming in, in about an hour so can y'all do something for me?"

"Ma'am?" They all answered on one accord.

"Lorraine, you can set up the table. Heidi you can take the ice trays out and put the ice cubes in the drinks. And velma you can watch this chicken."

They all quickly gathered around the kitchen, sank to sanitize and then went to work. But Ethel took notice of how weirdly her oldest was walking.

"Velma?" "Yes." She replied calmly.

"Can you come here for a second?" Velma stiffly put the fork down and grabbed the towel and walked to her mama to see what she wanted.

"Move the towel out the way little girl. You are trying to get over on me. I have told you time and time again that trousers on a Sunday aren't appropriate." She scolded Velma. And gave her a look that could kill.

"You're blessed that we have folks coming over for Sunday dinner because I can give you an ear full about right now." Agitated, Ethel walked past Velma and went to the storage room to grab her more supplies for the dinner. She had bigger fish to fry then worrying about a dress code.

Meanwhile David had just arrived with company of course. He ran upstairs to his room while little Jimmy took off his hat hanging it up on the hooks near the front door. He Cooley slicked back his mane and through his cigar in the nearest trash can. He was going to go into the kitchen but before he could step foot in the room Ethel caught him.

"Ahh ahh!" She teased. He playfully rolled his eyes and sighed. "Now where were you this morning? I don't recall you being in the congregation this morning." She challenged Jimmy up and down.

"Well I got off work last night and slept pretty late mama." Jimmy answered, scratching the back of his neck. Ethel wasn't his biological mother or anything of that sort but she was a mother figure in his life since his own mom was really young and skipped town to go live with her boyfriend who was an heroin addict. Little Jimmy had it hard along with his siblings, the Howard boys. They were young, strapping and handsome. But to most people they seemed dangerous and a defeated cause. Not to the waters though.

"Well you just go sit down in the living room and make yourself comfortable and me and the girls will have dinner ready in no time." It was a demand not a Suggestion. He sprawled out on the sofa and waited until David came back. David had put on His favorite shirt and some blue jeans, and he had grabbed his football.

"Aye man you wanna go outside?" He had already grabbed the door, throwing the ball up and catching it.

"Yeah let's go." Jimmy quickly agreed, hopping off the couch. But not before David's older sister and often pain in the butt interfered."David mama is gonna get you. She wants everybody in the house because dinner's gonna start soon." Velma nagged. She had come from the kitchen wearing an apron and wiping the flour on the side of her legs.

"Velma, Jimmy and I are just gonna be in the front yard. Mind your business." She glared at him as if she could burn a hole into his face.

"You mind your tone little boy." She retorted as she turned to walk away. Sarcastically, Jimmy jumped in to bother her a little bit.

"Hey, you too miss Velma." She didn't even think about him being there. For years he and her brother were just close and even if she didn't really care for him they had grown close like a family.

"Bye jimmy." She lastly said. She strutted her way back to the kitchen as the two other girls started to giggle.

Jimmy sucked his teeth watching her walk back into the kitchen. He smirked once he saw flour on the back of her yellow pin stripe trousers.

"What y'all laughing so hard about?" Velma softly asked.

"Bye Jimmy" Lorraine mocked and repeated.

"He can really leave, if he's gonna be that obnoxious." She was stressed. It was getting close to the time Lady Waters said dinner would be ready. The reverend hadn't even made it back yet. And uncle Julius hadn't made it back either. The stress of a Sunday dinner was to be compared with giving the queen of England a ball. The boys went on outside to play while dinner had just been finished. The reverend came in right on time just as if he had a timing device on him.

"Well hello everyone." The girls came rushing out the kitchen to hug their daddy.

"Good afternoon reverend waters." Lorraine greeted. Julius came packing behind him and took off his fedora. "Afternoon ladies." Julius winked putting his toothpick in his mouth.

"Hey Julius." They all said.

"My my my, Lorraine you've grown beautifully." David's uncle was quite the flirt but he meant no harm. He liked making people feel good about themselves. He remembers watching the vixen children when he was around ten. And now he could obviously see Rainy had grown into a beautiful young lady.

"Thanks brother Julius." She grinned, now blushing. She ran back into the kitchen and the girls followed.

"There's no use to waiting around anymore. The food has been ready for about 30 minutes now. Don't let it get cold." Velma commented when her mother came floating through the kitchen.

"I reckon so." Says Ethel. "Dinner is ready!" She yells for the whole house to hear. The girls waited and were propped up by the foyer. David and little Jimmy overheard and started fighting each other for seats.

"Well I sure hope assistant minister vixen gets here, looks like these boys got a pretty big appetite." Reverend water teases. He looked at the boy's big eyes. "There's more than enough." Ethel laughs.

"Girls come on and sit down at the table." He saw the girls waiting and was ready for the feast to start.

The girls did as he said.

"Now everyone bow their heads and hold each other's hands." He demanded. While everyone was getting situated he asked little Jimmy to give grace.
"James, will you do us the honor of saying grace?"
The whole table was silent. You could hear Velma giggling.
"He don't know how to pray." She whispered looking at Heidi. Little Jimmy felt discouraged. "Yeah reverend she's right, you know I-"
"Makes me no never mind, I want you to bless the food, son." Jimmy was basically family too. The reverend didn't approve of his lifestyle but he really cared about him seeing the rough life he had. The reverend glared at his daughter Velma. Sometimes she could be too self righteous for her own good.
"I can do that sir... father thank you for this delicious food that ma waters has made and thank you for the waters family, I ask that you bless it, in your name I pray amen." He quickly said and then gave an exasperated sigh.
"Amen!" The reverend encouraged looking at him proudly. Velma just sat back in her chair sulking.
"Can you pass the collard greens please?" Jimmy asked with a smirk on his face.
"There right there ,your hands are working, boy." She scoffed.
"Velma." Ethel gave her a disapproving look.
"I could have sworn y'all act like siblings and I never gave birth to him,"Ethel commented.
"Everyone enjoy the food, I've gotta start cleaning." She removed her cloth from her lap and immediately waltzed to the kitchen area to clean the dishes. Julius and David and the reverend conversation while Heidi and Lorraine talked about their affairs Velma helped her mother in the kitchen. And little

Jimmy took notice. He followed her into the kitchen and waited for First Lady waters to come out.

Velma was cleaning the counters with a rag and a spray bottle with yellow gloves on. She rubbed them harshly. "You know blue isn't a flattering color on you." Jimmy teased.

"What are you talking about? Go away." She dismissed him.

"Should've seen your face when the reverend asked me to pray. You turned blue." Velma stopped for a moment and folded her arms.

"I did not. Besides daddy knows you ain't a Christian got no business praying where we eat. We are liable to have food poisoned because your prayers bounced from the ceiling." She joked. She is half way serious though. "Look I believe in God, I just do things differently than y'all. Y'all sanctimonious folks. Can't drink this, can't eat that, can't watch this , can't say that and all the other BS. And then soon you can't live the life God intended for you to live. We just see different is all."He argued. He grabbed a dish and started drying it with a towel.

"Well I see why you are thinking that way. With all that street talk you are doing and your lady friends. I suppose life like that is fun. But I don't think God wants us to live that way." He giggled at her assumptions. Yes, the Howard boys had their ways. They were kind and quiet ladies men. But if you messed with them you had another thing coming.

"Maybe Velma maybe. But you worry about you college girl... and I worry about me." He said to her cut and dry. "Well good just good. Worry about you and stay away from my brother. He doesn't need to get involved in your thuggish ways." 'A thug?' He thought. Sure he could be wild sometimes but he didn't think that made him a thug.

"Me and your brother have been friends since day one and that ain't changing." He lastly said before handing her the last dried dish. He laughed dryly as he began to leave the kitchen.

Velma stood there baffled as he walked out and joined the rest of the family in their activities. She could never figure out why she was so pressed about little jimmy. He just got under her skin and the more he came around the more the ugly side of her showed.

**Chapter 3**

**'Heidi'**

"Heidi! When you go out today, get my butter at the store." My adoptive mother yelled from downstairs. I'm Heidi Jamison. I know it's peculiar because I call David and Velma my brother and sister but the truth is, I've grown up with them. They've been the only family I've known my whole life. When I was 3 years old my parents went on a missionary trip to Africa. Momma was a white woman and daddy a colored man. I don't have to begin to tell you how much trouble that is in the states. My momma was a Quaker and my dad a minister just like uncle David, but these days I find myself calling him Dad. I remember what they look like and how they smelt. I remember the smell of butterscotch and cologne my dad possessed. I

always sat in his lap and followed my mom around in church and the kitchen. When they got married it stirred such an uproar that they had to stay in New York. Until Africa that is...
I slung my purse over my shoulder and grabbed David's thin jean jacket.
"Don't forget choir practice is at 4:00 clock Heidi." David mentioned.
"And why are you wearing a jacket in this weather? Which just happens to be my jacket." David asked, grinning.
I wasn't really wearing it. I just wanted to cover my arms a little bit. You see, I have eczema. My skin gets all itchy and dry, then it flakes up. It shows on my arms and you know I'm 'high yella'.
"I'm just playing." David finished brushing past me and walking out the door with my uncles keys. You know I get it that I'm not their real biological daughter but I sure wish they'd give me a car. I'm 20 years old riding a bike through town. I ran down the front door steps of the house and hopped on my bike that was leaning on the fence. "Ahh shucks," I snapped. I scuffed my bobo sneakers on the pavement. The sneakers that mama waters hate so much. She should know that thousands of girls in America are wearing them by now. When I was riding through the neighborhood, I drove past the Hudson's house, the Lawry's and even Lorraine's home. It took at least 10 minutes to get into town.

Piggly wiggly was just down the road 'gotta get butter, gotta get butter' I thought. Every time I go into town I get nervous because The green brothers are always standing outside near the department store. I can only imagine their up to no good as usuals I decided to park my bike by piggly wiggly bike station.

And before I could get to the door Alvin started cruising in his 56 ford. He rolled his window down and threw out his cigarette bud. "Hey honey." I assumed he was talking to me but I kept walking and he kept cruising. "Now Heidi you best stop now you know I'm talking to you."

"Hey Alvin." I said quietly. The greens were extremely flirtatious and annoying. Not at all like the Howard boys. Especially since they left the Church of Christ temple . They caused turmoil in the neighborhood. And the church community. "That's better, what are you doing in town alone?" He slyly asked. Why does he need to know what I'm doing?It's my business. "Getting some things for my mama." I cut him short.
I watch Alvin dig into the front pocket of his jacket.

"Tell mama Waters, it's my pleasure." He says handing me a 100 dollar bill fold.
"Al- I can't accept this ,here." I gave the money back to him. He looked up at me with a scowl.
"That's okay I respect that, just know I'll be coming back for you sweet red bone. He retorts in a low chuckle, rolling his window back up and driving off.  "Finally." I said aloud with relief. I had to get that butter and other things for mama. Ever since high school Alvin Green has been trying to get with me. He's not my type though. And the way he comes at me... not exactly romantic. He creeps me out and my theory is he doesn't like me, he's just obsessed with how light I am. And I'm so tired of the color struck people in this town.

Later on I had finally got the butter and started trying to get back to the house before it got late. The truth is when I'm out and about I do more than run errands. I go to the library, the park and the dress shop on the corner. Mama keeps her dresses in tip top shape and there's no need to go to Burlington when we have the best seamstress in town, sister Albertina. "Heidi! beautiful girl!" she exclaims. "What brings you by the shop this afternoon?" "Hi sister Albertina, here just to see how the dress process is going." I giggled. "Well it's right in my office on that ugly mannequin. had to take it in because your mama has been losing some weight, her shape is to die for." sister Albertina was in her 60s and a short stocky woman. She was responsible for the church looking like a fashion show and she also made hats. legend has it that Mahalia Jackson got her dress made by Albertina because her personal seamstress was sick. Mama also did some beautiful work, but being busy with her First Lady duties and opening up a community day care hindered her. "Well here it is, yellow seems to be in right now. I'll have it ready tomorrow." she said lastly as I walked out the office. The dress was stunning. "Thanks sister Albertina" "you're welcome sweetheart, always a pleasure when working for my favorite customer lady Ethel." she smiled and bid me a farewell. It was almost time for rehearsal.

Yes, I can sing. I aint no Aretha Franklin though. I quickly rode to the house and dropped the requested items so mama could get started on dinner and then I ran back out.

"pass me not o gentle savior, hear my humble cry..." I heard as I walked up the steps. 'crap I am late. I tiptoed behind brother

Eugene the choir director and stood behind Lorraine. I could feel the disapproving stare from David on the organ.

I looked across the room at him and he was shaking his head. "Nice of you to join us, sister Heidi." Eugene adds. not only was he scolding me but the whole choir was too with their silent glares. "But you came in right on time, come down closer where I can see." I did not know what was going on. "Minister David, hand her the microphone." "what? why?" brother Eugene laughs before he answers me. "you're singing on Sunday Heidi." 'kill me now.' I thought. We practiced three songs and then the one song I was supposedly leading. Then by the time it was 6:30 Eugene let us out.
I watched him pack his things into a leather briefcase with staff music and lyric sheets. "Brother Eugene.." I started. I got nervous and began to twiddle with my thumbs. "Please don't make me sing on Sunday. you'd be doing yourself a disservice. I'm not that good of a singer." I pleaded.

The truth is I have a horrible stage fright. I remember we did a Christmas play and I was a sheep. I could not even make a sheep noise without running off stage and crying. " Now Miss Heidi, you chose your own fate when you showed up to rehearsal late. let me be the one to judge if you're a good singer or not." he said lastly, slinging his briefcase to his right hand. He waltzed out the building. David could not wait to annoy me because he was laughing as soon as I turned around. he patted my shoulder "I told you to not be late." he's always saying 'I told you so' me and David are the same age and I'm older by a few months but he swears up and down that he is like my big brother.

"What are you and the band about to get into?" I asked if I know they are likely to stay here and shed. shedding is when a group of musicians get together and just groove and play music. It's like a creativity spot. "Me and the fellas are gonna stay back a little while longer and little Jimmy stopping by too." "Jimmy can come to rehearsal but can't come to service?" I asked aloud. David only chuckled "you sound like Velma, just get off his case. I'm trying to slowly convince him to come." The only thing you can convince Jimmy to do is a few things and they are not polite to say.

"yeah alright." I tease. David walks me out of the church but instead we take the back door. the one reverend waters take when the deacon thinks too many people are bothering him. "It's really not smart for you to be riding out by yourself, girl." " David I can take care of myself, don't need you holding my hand" I scoffed. "I'm just saying it's dangerous especially when it's gonna be dark soon." "It's 7 and the sun is still out, what danger boy?" I nearly rolled my eyes before Jimmy came to the back with us. "hey what's happening? How are you Heidi?" he greeted David and then gave me a hug. "the fellas ready to start jamming, they are waiting on you." he informed him.

"right right, I'll catch you later Heidi... be safe." It wasn't long before he went off. I ran down the steps and looked in our backyard. There was a car parked by the tree and a tall white man smoking a cigar. well maybe not a man but a young man kind of boyish. His collared shirt was unbuttoned and the wind from the trees were blowing through his auburn brown hair. He had a camera slung over his neck. He looked at me and I looked at him.

"Excuse me, miss?" when I crawled on my bike I suddenly heard him call out to me. I started paddling as fast as I could .white men are nothing but trouble. Besides, he could have been a policeman for all I know.

"miss?" he yelled to get my attention. I figured if he went to such great lengths to get my attention. it was probably rude to ignore the man.

I sighed and rode my bike to where he was. "yessir?" "look I've been burning rubber for a couple of days and I know I'm in North Carolina but can you tell me what town this is, you dig?" 'Burning rubber? dig?' I thought. The man sounded like one of those Italian mobsters from the movies me and Velma snook and watched when we were little.

"Beverdille, you lost? Greensboro is 30 minutes up the road." "No, this is perfect..." he says looking around. He places his cigarette behind his ear. "And uhh do you know Reverend waters?" I just looked away. "why? is he in some sort of trouble?" "nah 'I'm not the police or anything, the only thing I'm interested in is reporting back to my boss." 'He's a reporter, that explained the camera.' "you're a reporter?" I asked.

"Something like that." the white man smirks.

He took out his hand to shake mine. "I'm John. John Ferrari." I am reluctant to grab his hand in return. "Well Mr. Ferrari, you may be on the wrong side of town." I confess hopping back on my bike.

"No worries, I am on the right side, if the map and address I was given serves me right. And Mr. Ferrari is my father's name. You can just call me John." he says. I Suspect he may have only been a few years older than me. But it was custom in the south to call any white gentleman by their surname and to put a title in front of it. If we didn't, other whites could suggest you were being too common. And they also thought you were an uppity colored person.

We could not be on the same level as them. I've watched people my age call my grandparents by their first names. They referred to them as boy, gal. it didn't really matter. But it definitely burned my skin to see the people in my community, so worthy and deserving of honor, be dishonored.

" I think I'll stick with calling you Mr. Ferrari, Good day mr. Ferrari." I yell back hurrying on my cycle. "you too uhh-" he struggled to find out what to call me.

"Heidi!" I answered.

## Chapter 4

**'Velma'**

Heidi didn't come back to the house til 8:09. She had mama worried and daddy was about to take a shotgun to somebody. And David, well let's just say I'm covering for him. Because if it gets too late he'll never be able to leave this house and will be restricted to choir rehearsals as extracurricular activities. 'Poor David' meanwhile I've been at the house helping mama cook and trying to keep daddy's hypertension down.

I'm velma. I'm 22 years old so I guess that makes me a woman, right? If only it were that simple. People look at me and automatically think I have it together and that I'm judgemental just because I am the eldest and help my parents with the church. They can say all they want but I've seen people come in and out of my life and in and out of my daddy's church. They hurt him badly, but you would never know that by looking at him. And they never liked my mama. My parents fed people, and put the clothes on their back. Even let some people stay at our house for months. But what did those people do? Leave the church or worse steal from the collection plate. And I guess you could say I'm protective over my brother David. That's because I know there's some snakes trying to take him down. I love my brother and I love Heidi too. Heidi is my sister-cousin, her being born from my mother couldn't make us closer. We don't always see eye to eye but if someone bothers her I won't be acting like a Christian woman then. Nobody messes with my family.

Just as I turn over to fall asleep I hear someone knocking at my window. It startled me a bit. But I know who it is. It's David. "Boy, are you crazy? it's after midnight." I whisper. "I know! Can you open the front door?" He exclaims. I bet he was out with little Jimmy. I throw on my robe and quietly tip toe down stairs to open the door. "They up?" He asked. I silently shake my head. "It was the Howard boys wasn't it?" I asked, disappointed.

"No, me and the fellas were shedding all night and we went over the time." He says matter of factly.
"Shedding my behind." I tease and feel myself yawn.
"Good night, I'm going to bed."
"Velma I owe you one."
"Mhmm."
That morning the sun came up and I remember I had forgotten to put the window seal back down. In the south mosquitoes run rampant and I felt one biting the flesh on my neck. Today was Saturday and that meant it was cruising time. Lots of young people went cruising in the town and had picnics. It was lots of fun. Me and Heidi did it at least once a month. And the key was to dress cute and make lunch and just go. Of course I'm taking David's car.

I took the rollers out of my hair after I finished bathing and then I moisturize my face, put some powder on and used a pinch of eye liner. Lastly, putting on my lipstick. I wasn't going alone when we were cruising. Rule number one, ladies never travel alone; they take at least two of their friends. And That would be Heidi and Lorraine for me. I was going to drag Heidi even if she didn't want to come.
I put on my white pleated shorts and then my pinstripe camisole. I lastly put my pearls in
my ears. When I'm finished I grab my mini purse putting a few dollars in. In case we run into some trouble. "Heidi come on, we're going to Lorraine's" I say, knocking on her door. She opens the door looking exhausted.
"You're not wearing that are you?" I scowl.
"Be glad I'm coming at all." She answered, rolling her eyes.

"Fine, just don't wear that big ole hat. We're not going to church today."

"Girl, I know that. It's just my style." She argues. "Please just take that thing off." She takes it off, tossing it on her bed.

See I don't get why she's always trying to hide it. She has a head full of hair. Pretty, curly hair.

"Yeah just wear it out like that." I comment. She sighs and we run down the stairs. I grab David's key from the bowl that's sitting by the door. Then I take out my scarf and wrap it around my chin and hair. Then I won't forget my white sunglasses. We cruise down the street a little bit before we arrive at the Vixen's residence. I get out of the car to ring the doorbell. Sister vixen opens it and greets me at the door. "Velma? What are you doing here sweetheart?" She questions.

"Hey sister vixen, me and Heidi are here for Lorraine. We are going to the 'Boro' today." I explain.

"Greensboro, rainy ain't mention nothing like that, lemme go get her." She says before leaving the door momentarily. 'Lord help her.' I think. Rainy is my best friend back home. She's turning 20 soon and her parents never let her go out. It just so happens that I'm the pastor's daughter and I get to take her out. If it was anyone else she'd be locked up in the house like Rapunzel.

Rainy comes out to the door dressed in a collared shirt and a flared pink skirt with chuck Converse sneakers. Her hair was tied in a ribbon and her bangs swept to the side. She looked like she belonged on an American bandstand.

"Hey let's go." She says quickly. "I'm Sorry mama it slipped my mind to tell you." "Mhmm." Her mom says as she kisses her cheek.

"Y'all be safe out there." Her mom lastly said before shutting the door. But we could all see her looking through the window.

"Thank goodness you came!" Lorraine sighed in relief. "Why do you say that girl?" "My mom was gonna let George come over to keep me company."
I and Heidi started giggling. "You mean Mother Johnson's Grandson?" "Yes that one, he asked my daddy if he could court me. He's almost 30 and he's already balding. Just eww." She said disgustedly.
"Now are you saying you don't like older men?" Heidi teased. Me and Heidi often picked on Lorraine about our uncle Julius; he wasn't exactly old but not our age either. He flirts with everything that has a pulse but we recall Lorraine having a huge crush on him back when she was 14 and he went to the Korean War. A funny story is that Lisa, a girl who went to our church and was the women's youth department president, dated uncle Julius. And they were engaged, Lorraine used to call our house to talk to uncle Julius and warn him of the mistake he was making by marrying Lisa. He just laughed. He kind of knew Lorraine had a crush. He saw it as endearing. We saw it as territorial. Now her crush is all gone but it's still funny to think about.
"No ma'am y'all know Julius is too old. That was just a silly crush."
"Well I don't know rainy, your mama and daddy are 15 years apart." I tease as we speed up on the road.
" aww hush that up those were the olden days." She says defending them.
I got my license 2 years ago because I needed it to travel back and forth between home and Greensboro on Sunday mornings.

But I haven't driven in awhile since summer started. It took 30 minutes to get there and soon we just started cruising down the street.

I had a list of things I wanted to do. Catch a moving picture and visit the department store and then maybe stop at Andy's for lunch. But all that wasn't gonna happen today. You see, the day before Sunday is very critical. I have to pick my dress out and iron it and then I have to do a facial before I go to bed. Then of course roll my hair up. Beauty is pain.

"When do you say the cruising start?" Heidi asked.

"It starts a little after noon." I answered

"I sure hope we see some cute guys out here today." Lorraine commented.

" Me too." Heidi says,shocking herself. When we got into the city I parked my car by Andy's restaurant. I already knew how this was gonna go. We couldn't eat inside because of the Jim Crow law. Y'all know how that goes. They don't want us touching them but I for one don't wanna touch them. For all I know  they could be dirty. My aunt on my daddy's side used to be a maid for rich white folks and she can tell you they were just unsanitary. Dog hairs on the furniture. They left dirty underwear in closets and drawers and they smelled like quarters. So it makes me no never mind.

Me and the girls had decided to order a burger and a shake and we were on our way.

"Hey I'm going to the department store." I told Heidi and Lorraine.

"For what?"  "My shoes for Sunday." I explained.

"Girl you got enough shoes, you probably got more than mama. Plus you know how prejudiced Mr. Walker is." The Walkers owned almost every store or franchise in Beverdille. Before the

sharecropping days they owned the acres and the people on it. That's where their attitude of entitlement came from. He won't let you try the shoes on." Heidi continues,this was true. I can't even count on my hands how many times we ran into racist all over town. And they felt they was doing us a favor by even serving colored folks.  Well they won't get this colored dollar. 'How about that.' I thought.
"You're right let's just sit here and drive." I suggested. And before we knew it cruising started. Everyone was beeping their horns at each other. And one particular gentleman had turned his stereo up in the car. He blasted lonely teardrops by Jackie wilson.
And what do you know? I spotted the Howard boys. I mentally rolled my eyes.
"Velma look!" Heidi said, pointing at jimmy.
"Didn't anyone ever tell you it's not polite to point?" I told her to grit my teeth. After the argument me and him had a few weeks ago, things were tense and more tense than usual. Before he was just that annoying guy that tagged along with David everywhere we went but now I'm worried that I may have actually hurt him by what I said. I know that I come off harsh, but I honestly mean well.
"The Howard boys are coming, they're behind us." Rainy whispers.
"And boo hoo. They're just like any other guy out here." I said and continued driving.
And it wasn't to my surprise because Jimmy stuck his head out of the car. His older brother Theo was driving instead. "Hey ladies!" He greeted me.
"Hey Little Jimmy." Heidi and Lorraine said in unison.

"I'm surprised by boy David ain't out here." He looked bewildered.
"Oh he slept in and he's probably gonna help daddy with the yard today." Heidi had filled him in on the details.
"And I supposed y'all taking his place huh?" He chuckled.
"Yeah you could say that." Rainy said.
"Is this one mute?" He joked. I could see him staring at me from the side of my face.
"Hello James." I spoke softly and I was nearly agitated. I moved my bangs from my eyes." Ohhh she speaks." I heard him and his brothers laughing in the car.
"Tell me, what are good Christian girls like yourself doing out here cruising? Man ain't there some rules in the Bible against that?" He teases. Little Jimmy dumps some of his cigarette ashes on the street while everyone is in traffic. "Jimmy,don't start, okay?" I look over at him, raising my eyebrows.
"What, you're afraid you're gonna actually have some fun? Why don't y'all come to the park in Greensboro all the chicks and fellas are gonna be having a ball. Ya dig?"
"Yeah I dig it jimmy!!" We heard some female holler in a car behind us. It was super awkward the way she tried to get his attention we all agreed silently to act like it didn't happen.
"Cool." He lastly said, rolling his window back up.
I wonder what the girls are going crazy over.
"I say we go and check it out." Lorraine suggested.
"Yeah I mean it couldn't hurt? Plus I heard some of your folks from a&t are gonna be there. Maybe even patty."
"Definitely not if Patty is gonna be there." I retorted.
"Who's patty?" "Patty is Velma's horrible roommate." Heidi snickers.

All of a sudden we run into this white man, he starts snapping pictures of people in vehicles. 'Is cruising illegal?' It gets mad silent in the car. I catch Lorraine and Heidi making eye contact. "What's going on?" I say looking behind me and stirring the wheel. "Nothing." Heidi answered. But she kept looking at Lorraine. And they looked at the man. "Uh uh y'all keeping something from me, who's that white man and why y'all keep looking at each other?"
"Tell her Heidi." Rainy encouragement. "He ain't hurt y-" I began to ask something but Heidi shook her head.
"No nothing like that, that man was at the church last night, said he came looking for daddy." She explained. But her eyes said something else. It was a look I'd never seen in Heidi's eyes before. A dangerous one. Now I can admit when someone's handsome, I'm not blind but a white man. Now that's a different territory.
"You better stop staring at him like that."
"I was not staring at him!" She argued.
"Yeah, alright."

I should have gone to the party but I always gotta be a goody two shoes. Maybe folks are right about me. Maybe I am boring. But as a pastor's daughter I have to think for more than just myself. Heidi is different , she can get away with anything and nobody will judge her. Rainy isn't the pastor's daughter but she's close enough. And even she wouldn't get treated as harshly as I would. Going to that party could mess up my father and mothers reputation.
"Did you girls have fun today?" Mama waters asked as me and Heidi settled in.
"Yes ma'am we had lots of it."

"Y'all weren't out there doing that cruising the news was talking about right?" She suspiciously asked.
"Now mama what would make you think that?" I hear David jump in the conversation.
'He's saving me' I guess that's the one he owes me. I run upstairs and finish bathing. I use this natural guac cream for my face. My mom put me onto it and then I rolled my hair. It was about 10:00 by the time I was finished. I heard someone ring the doorbell down stairs. 'Who could that be?' I thought. Mom and daddy were surely asleep so I tiptoed down stairs to open the door before my father would become startled. Or worse uncle Julius would have a fit

"Umm David is asleep." It was Jimmy. And then I realized I was standing in front of James Howard with green stuff all over my face. Ashamed I put my robe up to cover my face a bit.

"But you're not," he says.

"And you've got green stuff on your face." he chuckles lightly trying to touch my face, but then I create a barricade between my face and his hand.

"I didn't notice." I say rolling my eyes.
"Well if he's asleep just tell him don't forget about our plans."

"I am pretty sure he is, you know normal people are around this hour. But you can leave and get back to doing whatever you were doing with your ladies of the night." I teased. I halfway believed what I was saying though.

"I'm not that bad, quit fronting with me."
He looked at me, and then I looked at him. But then he decided it was best to let me go. We could quarrel another time. Jimmy wasn't so bad, he was my brother's best friend after all. But the sweet one I grew up with went to sunday school with, changed when we got to junior high. His mom running off with another man and his father being a drunk didn't help his cause. But I guess he turned out okay. But that's besides the point, I think he could be a bad influence on David Jr.

"Good night Jimmy." I lastly said closing the door on him with a teasing smile.

## Chapter 5

**'John Ferarri'**

The boss said he needed me, quickly. So I got up and ran to the office without so much of a thought of washing my face. The office was packed for some odd reason. Reporters were leaving the scene left and right. I could have sworn I saw Joe Louis in the press conference room with Tom Swavinsky.

I'm John Ferrari, I grew up in Rochester New York and when I say that most people aren't familiar with it. My family is Italian, hence my last name. My grandparents came to the states in the 20's and had my pops and then my pops got lucky and met another Italian kid that just so happened to live across the street. They got married and had me. Rochester isn't like

New York City or Long Island; it has a more down home or suburban feel. But yeah I'm that kid. I went to college and got a butt load of degrees that I can't even pay off the student loans. One thing I do know is that if I can't do anything else, I can sell a story.

"Ferrari! get your butt in here! " Ray was the chief and editor of times magazine, he ran a tight ship and only hired the best of the best. I started off as an intern here just a year ago but Ray is really riding me now since I am an actual employee.

"I was summoned?" Candy, an errand girl, giggled at my sarcasm. I slightly tilted my head looking inside of Ray's office. "get in here." he didn't give my joke the slightest attention. I grabbed my book bag and swung it over the chair that was right beside me. Ray's office was just how you'd imagine an editor and chief office to look, huge and almost set up like a lounge.

" Now kid ain't I got news for you, are you familiar with the NAACP?"  he asked. "is that the college negro fund sir?"  I wasn't so sure of where he was going with this"no, no, I mean close enough but this is the biggest colored organization in the United States."  "okay."

"so the daily news has bombed their chance of getting the story right because they insulted some people of color." The daily news was our competition, even though times had always been on the top it was our job to keep winning. "Dr. king is a negro man, he's a pretty young fella too. and we at New York  times want to get inside his head a bit. see what this movement is about." he finishes.

"Well that's just great Ray but most of the movement is in the south and we're up here." "exactly and the organization is set up in various places. the main place is the church."

"what are you getting at Ray?" "let me get to it kid." I see candy walking up to his desk to fill his cup with more coffee. He takes a sip of the new filled cup and places an ink pen behind his ear.

"what I am saying is, I want you on this paper. you've got the niche for impressive finds Ferrari. Now I've already gotten Nick to go to Alabama but you, I am sending you to a big church in North Carolina."

"what you trying to do, convert me?" Ray chuckled a bit. "that's very funny, I've always liked you. but do what you got to do. I'm sending you to Beverdille, a small town in North Carolina and from what they have told me the nearest city is Greensboro." he says. I look at him pondering. something like this could jump start my career as a journalist and photographer. yes, I do both.

my only problem is how could I get there? and how would I break this to my family that's so dependent on me? I delve so deep in my thoughts that I forget my boss is talking to me. "Ferrari, are you listening?" "uhh yeah, you want me to dig deep and find the heart of the movement."

"Correcto mundo" "But Ray I don't know the way things are for me at h-" he stopped me before I could say another word. "Are you saying you don't want this opportunity?" "No, I'm not saying that." I answered him, startled. "good because I have faith in you kid, and I think this could be your big break! Candy, get this kid a cup of coffee we have details to discuss." the door is slammed shut and my life would be changed forever.

"That night I went home and packed my bags. I was gonna take the airplane but all the seats were filled and there was no way I was taking the first class seats with my paycheck. So it was a road trip.

I slept in about two hotels before I could get into town and boy I tell ya, ain't nothing like southern hospitality. They say good morning and they shine your shoes. And the women are pretty too.
"Darling, could you hand me your coffee cup?" A stocky waitress with blonde hair asked. She was trying to refill my cup. As I looked at what I wanted to eat. "You know what you want yet baby?"
"Yes I do. I want the waffle, bacon and eggs combo. And what is soda?"
"Soda? Sir you know cola." Up north we call that soda pop."Oh yeah let me get one of those." She shakes her head smiling.
"Your order will be ready sir." I was now in Raleigh and from what I had heard, I was getting closer to my destination. The sign read ' you are now entering the town of Beverdille, welcome" the sign was wooden and the color from the letters

halfway chipped off. I saw something that I thought was just a folktale. Cotton fields. And then further down the road tobacco fields. I thought I was lost. It seemed like each side I looked at people were working in the fields. I stopped momentarily to ask a worker if I was or in the right place.

"Excuse me, can somebody tell me where the church of Christ temple is?" They all looked up at me with blank expressions. And they went back to picking tobacco. But one gentleman came to me. "Suh? You said church of Christ temple. Uhh you lookin fo the Reverend?" I instantly became aware of how different the dialect is in the south. "Yes, I'm looking for David Water's. " I said, looking at my notes. You see I was told that this church was holding a big conference pulling all big time churches from the south. And the keynote speaker was going to be Dr. king. "Well which one there's two of em reverend and then little David Jr." He chuckled, throwing his hoe on the ground and spitting out his chewing tobacco. "You must be a member of the church."

"No not hardly but my granddaughter sings in the choir. Listen if you need directions to the church it's just about 5 miles up the road make two lefts and then one right and you should be there."

"Thank you Mr-" "Buddy, buddy is just fine." He picked his hoe back up and tipped his straw hat towards me. I got back in the car making my next few minutes to the church. It was hardly dark. But that was just because it was daylight saving time. When I arrived I heard a lot of singing and clapping and I was confused because I thought church was for Sunday's. I mean unless you were a seventh day Adventist. A girl came out of the back and I just had to know where the reverend was. But she wasn't a big help. Good thing I parked under the tree. That night I saw no sign of rain or any sign of burglary so I got my sleeping bag and my tent I bought from the store. I went to sleep.

The next day I woke up to the sound of honking horns from the automobiles on the street.
"Are you okay mister?" A little colored girl ran up to me waving her hands over my eyes. I felt the wind so I opened them. And then I sat up.
I smiled at her. She looked about 5 and she had chubby cheeks and curly frizzy hair that was in a bow. "Hi." I said gently. Suddenly her eyes widened and she became startled and ran away to a house that was right across from the church. It was the cutest thing to see.
I chuckled a little, rubbing the crust out of my eyes. Frankly the sound of the horns on the street were irritating me. I got out of my tent and took off my letterman jacket as it was probably 1000 degrees.
The car that rolled up was a 1960 red mustang. And it's not even 1959 yet. Elvis Presley's hound dog busted through the stereo. A girl rolled down her window. She was pale and had freckles and her hair was red and curly and it hung loosely out the car.
"Are you by any chance lost?" She was yelling loud enough for me to hear her look over to a girl beside her who I assumed was her friend, to turn the radio down.
"No, I am found! Thank you." I got my toothbrush out the trunk and looked in the mirror and brushed them as the girl watched. "That was cute." She snickered

"Can I help you?" I was confused as to why they were still parked on the side of the road and looking at me. Where I'm from, if a man is outside alone sleeping in his car or by his car everyone just minds their business. They might leave him a dollar or two but they don't go up to just bother the man.
"Looks like you're the one who needs help. Don't ya know where you are?"
"Yeah church of God temple."
"Duh but you're in the colored part of town. There's a motel down the road. And if you can't afford it my home is open for you to stay in till you can get up off your feet." It seemed the lady thought I was in a bad circumstance. And from the outside I could see why.
"My name is Emma Walker and you are?" She took her hand out to shake my hand. I guess making connections in town wouldn't be so bad. So far everyone I met has run away from me.
"John Ferrari."
"Well it's a pleasure to meet such a fine gentleman..." she pursed her thin lips.
"Remember you may want to get out of the colored part of town. They are not accustomed to us being here. You know if you need help stop by the walker pharmacy."
"I'll keep that in mind." "See ya Mr. Ferrari" her and her friend in the car giggled and then drove off.
I waved, forgetting that my toothbrush was still in my hand. Looks like I was going to have more than a conference to write about. It had only been a day and a few hours and the southern lifestyle had already grown on me.

## Chapter 6

### 'That strange white boy'

Sunday service had ended and just like always, everyone was eating at the reverend's house. The Waters family always opened their home for others. And they enjoyed the company. While everyone was eating the Reverend heard a knock at the door.
"Hold on saints for just one moment, it seems we have a visitor." He cleaned his hands off on a napkin and stood up. He walked past the foyer and near the stairs to the house front entrance door.
He then opened the door.
"How can I help you, young man?" At first he was frightened to see the auburn colored hair ,white gentleman standing on his front porch. But he maintained his decorum.
 "Good evening, I was told that this was the address of the reverend waters home?" The white male visitor questioned. Now as ambitious Ferrari was he should have known that it isn't smart to show up to black peoples homes unannounced. "I am he. Do we need to talk outside? I don't want to worry my members."
"No worries reverend, just here to set the record straight. I hear you are hosting a conference at your church this summer."
"Well yes..." all of this was true but what did this have to do with him?

"The SCLC and the NAACP are collaborating for an event and they found it fit to be my church. I have one of the biggest influences in this region so they felt that it would be smart to use my ministry."
"Will Dr. King be present?" "...."
The reverend stared at him with a blank gesture.
"I'm sorry I can't disclose that kind of information sir."
"John." "What?"
"My name is John." He answered.
"Well I'm sorry John but I can't have that. The last thing we want is press and camera crews flashing the man. He works really hard and has a family back home. We aren't gonna put more on him." The reverend stood his ground. This wasn't some sensational story that the press could twist in their own words. Or for people to wonder why Dr. king was visiting Carolina. Things hadn't been the same for him since he got out of the hospital. It was reported that a lady stabbed him with a mail cutter. And he was hospitalized. If he would've sneezed the whole operation would have been over and he would have died. He's been resting with his family but many guessed that he was eager to get back out and fight for justice. And that the show must go on.
"please you've got to tell me Reverend! This is something I'm sure all colored people would want to know about especially in a small town like this." And John was on to something. Beverdille hadn't got much recognition except for their indulgent Christmas decorations every year and how much crops they produced. And maybe they just started getting recognition for Reverend Waters' church but that wasn't nearly enough compared to cities like Raleigh, Charlotte or Greensboro.

"You've got to earn your report, son." The reverend answered softly. It had been a long time since John had heard an older man speak to him in that way. Things just weren't like that back home.

Soon John left but what he didn't know was that Heidi was spying on their conversation. She was upstairs looking through her window.

Days had gone on and people in the Beverdille community were talking up a storm about Ferrari. They called him the strange white boy. They never met a white man who spoke to them as if he were their equal. Or a man that played patty cake with their children. He was strange but strange in a good way. He became liked. People were still cautious of him because that was just the way of the times. But it was nice to not have a white man coming around thinking he was gonna bust your door down or hang boys on trees with ropes, for a change.

David and some of the youth were at bible study at the church. Kids were really confused as to why a white man's car and tent was sitting under the tree.

"Minister David, I think that white man is the feds."

"Oh hush up Lamont. The Bible says to judge ye not, remember that?" All of the kids giggled. Their youth group was mostly kids from the age 12 to 18. And David wasn't too far from their age.

"The boy could be right tho." He murmured under his breath to Lorraine who was now leading a woman's youth group. She rolled her eyes playfully and shook her head. "What are you doing out here tonight Rainy?" He questioned. He put his bible on the pew and turned away from the kids he was teaching, who were talking loudly.

"Why minister David, I'm teaching women's bible study. You do know that women exist in the Bible too?" She sassed. David bit his lips.
"Yeah. Of course. What scripture are you in? Proverbs 31?" He grabbed her clipboard that was laced with notes and multiple verses on them.
His face lit up because she had things up there that he'd never think about.
"I'd figure you say that. Proverbs 31 is a great scripture but I've prepared different things for this quarter and for the young girls. I prefer for them to take baby steps and learn about the important women in the Bible. Like Ruth, Esther, Deborah or even Virgin Mary." She explained.

"I see. You'd make an excellent teacher, sister Lorraine." He commented. She didn't expect for him to give her a compliment. She looked up at him, her eyelids flickered softly.
"Thank you." Lorraine responded she grabbed her notes from David and strides towards the other side of the room to be with her girls. Heidi watched them from the side propped up against the wall. She walked up to David who was momentarily in a gaze.
"I see the way you look at her." He heard her voice come from behind him.
"Huh?" "Don't huh me." He laughed waiting for her explanation. "You need to tell Lorraine how you feel, you've been crushing on her since you were 12." She joked.
"I did not have a crush on her when I was 12." He denied making a face as if what Heidi said was absurd.

"Come on now. Me and Velma knew it was you that wrote her that secret love song. That she keeps in her room."
"She keeps it in her room?" Heidi was fishing for information she didn't know if it was really from him.
"So it was from you!" Excited Heidi raised her volume. "Listen David I've seen the way girls look at you and you are a handsome young man and you got a way with girls. I just think the girl should be Rainy."
"Now go." She pushed him toward the other side of the room. Heidi and David had a close relationship as well; they were the same age. But they always butted heads about who was older. Technically Heidi was older but David held it over her head about how she was a girl and he was a guy.
She looked out the window and decided to go outside and see if John was there. And behold he was there. He was setting up his tent for the night.

"Are you just gonna stay out here every night?"
He was silent.
"You know mosquitoes are really bad down here." Still he didn't answer Heidi.
She got frustrated and started walking the other way. John noticed and smirked. He took his tie off and threw it over the tent.
"Is that your way of saying hi?" He voiced.
Heidi sucked her teeth and froze. "Hey John." "Hey Heidi." "I saw you the other week cruising."
"Oh yeah? What were you doing out there anyways?"
"The real question is what were you doing miss Heidi?" He looked up at her crouching and playing with a nail. "Hanging with friends. Not that it's any of your business."

"Any of my business." He murmured while continuing to set up. "You're right, you're right. But what brings you by?"
"I heard you earlier this week. Outside my house."
"Wait, you're a Waters?" He had finally realized she was related to the Reverend.
"Yeah if you don't count my being adopted." Heidi tittered.
"Makes sense as to why you thought I was a cop. I mean what's up with you people?"
"You people?" She retorted.
"Wait, I didn't mean it that way." John retracted. "Well then what did you mean then? Us people? Colored people, negroes? *Niggers* Mr. Ferrari." She further instigated. Heidi fumed and crossed her arms.
"Woah, that's not what I meant at all. Come inside please, I can tell you everything you need to know."
"I don't think I want to." She answered. "I'm a gentleman. I never impose on women. So suit yourself. " he shrugged while crawling further into the tent.
"Fine." She dragged. He grabbed Heidi's hand and she crawled in. John had covers that surfaced the ground. A bar that he had his tie and jackets on. He lifted off his white t- shirt causing Heidi's eyes to be wide open. She immediately covered them. He turned around to her only to laugh at how innocent she seemed. He started placing photographs on his sheets and brought out his flashlights.
He brought light to them.
"Look." Heidi turned her head looking at the photos in awe.
"You took these?" He nodded his head.
He took pictures of people in fields ,people cruising ,and people shopping in town. He even got photos of folks talking outside of the church.

"You know it's something about the way the people live down here. The fellas, the ladies. It's all so idiosyncratic." He explained passionately.

"That's one of the silliest things I've ever heard. Poetic though." Heidi teased picking up another photo.

She noticed that it was further down the row with girls sitting in an automobile and a girl's long curly tresses stretching down the passenger seat. She knew it was her.

"Is that me John?" "Let me see..."

"It appears to be." He answered while his eyes smiled. She couldn't help but notice his strange northern accent.

"Where are you from? Cause you're not from here." She knew there was no way he was from the south speaking that way.

"Obviously." He joked. "But I'm from Rochester, New York."

"Hmm." "Familiar place huh?"

"Yeah I lived there as a little girl." "How? I thought you lived here in Beverdille?"

"That's a long story for another day. What about you? What's your story? What brings you here to Beverdille? She asked.

"Well for starters I'm here on assignment to write about the civil rights movement that's just beginning and I'm here because word has it that Dr. King is speaking at a convention down here."

"What do you know about Dr. king?" Heidi said. She assumed white people just thought he was a young colored man starting trouble, when all colored folk wanted the same opportunities as their white counterparts.

"I know he's a good man." John argued. Something turned on in Heidi. She was slowly starting to see the strange white boy in a different light. She knew something was different about him.

"he is." Heidi finished. "What's it like back home? You have a family? A wife?" She had a hunch but she wasn't really sure.
"Want my driver license number too?." He said flippantly. "I'm sorry I didn't mean it that way. Just curious."
"Nah, it's cool. But for the record I have my parents that live back home. But I live in an apartment suite. And sorry to disappoint you but no wife."
"I find that hard to believe." She snickered.
"What about you? What do you do besides church?"
"Very funny Ferrari. But I go to A&T University and I'm thinking about being a lawyer."
"Hmm I didn't take you for the law type. I was thinking more artistic." He said putting his palm on his chin.
"Well you can stop reading me cause you're wrong." She sassed.
"What about you? boyfriend?" He soon took out a cigarette and a lighter.
She laughed.


"What? It's a serious question." He smiled.
"No. I don't have time for a boyfriend."
"Well that's a bummer." He said putting his cigarette lighter back in his pocket. "Why?" Heidi asked.
"Cause you make time for what you want."
"Yeah well I guess that makes two of us."
"Who said I didn't want a wife or a girlfriend?"
"Well you did Mr. Ferrari you said you don't have a wife and your kind, I'm sure has many lady friends." Heidi delicately explained.

"I guess you've got me figured out then miss Heidi."

"I guess I do." As strange as he seemed she couldn't help but to conjure up a fascination with him.

She thought she was crazy to be sitting in a tent alone with a man. And even crazier with a white man.

"Are all the girls here pretty as you are?" He asked. She was sure he was trying to get a rise out of her. She was startled by his forwardness but didn't let it show on her face.

Heidi looked at him, slightly rolling her eyes. But she couldn't hide her attraction for too long because she blushed. Her cheeks raised and they turned a rosy red.

"Good night Ferrari." She rushed and climbed out the tent. She nervously ran back in the church she knew David and the others were looking for since bible study had probably been over for some time.

'What was I thinking? A white man's tent? Really Heidi' she thought. She knew John Ferarri was an attractive man but she was way out of her head if she was gonna try to pursue anything with him.

She had no reason to believe anything solid or good could come out of a situation like that.

## Chapter 7

**'Sugar Rays'**

a month in...

Summer had its way for the most part, things were starting to make sense in the town of Beverdille. even for the Waters kids. it seemed like their life was different then the other young people in town. the others could party to the break of dawn without so much of a thought. David, Velma and Heidi sure couldn't do that. It was Saturday night and Sam Cooke came to town. When he came to visit he liked stopping by that old shack on Preston street. It was an old joint that played records and hosted some of the best artists. as raggedy as the place looked it sure lived up to its hype. The joint was called Sugar Rays; it opened up in the 30s and since then it kept getting renovated.

Saturday the boys got to talking and they made a bet that if David didn't ask to keep Lorraine company at the church picnic he would have to break curfew and go to the juke joint with the fellas. "I ain't studying what yall got to say. something like this is a delicate matter."

"delicate matter?! or is it you afraid she's gonna turn around and reject you?" Stacy, one of David's friends replied. David didn't utter one word and the whole group bursted in laughter. They all hopped in Jimmys vehicle and headed to the church picnic, if they would have stayed any longer lady Ethel would have bugged them so she could get help with bringing dishes. Meanwhile the girls were at the church setting up the picnic. They even helped with making the major dishes. Cornbread, potato salad, and baked macaroni and cheese. Of course they

let the big dog up to lady waters. No one could fry a batch of chicken the way she could. Heidi began to grunt and sweat.
"Can you believe they got us out here working like we were some slaves?"
"Ughh what are you complaining about now?" Velma Asked wiping the sweat from her brow.
..."it's the Lord's work."
"Sure it is". Heidi sassed. "Girl calm down, it's not that serious, we are just serving food." Lorraine interjected walking past them with a platter of honey bun cakes and lemon ones wrapped in Saran Wrap.
"If it's the lord's work, shouldn't this picnic be feeding the hungry?" Heidi pointed at sister Johnson who didn't look so hungry. She was a stocky woman and made sure she got a plate and her seconds, and then some. Velma started chuckling and slapped the back of Heidi's shoulder.
"Y'all ain't right." Lorraine grinned.
While the girls served plates to members and visitors sister Gracie served lemonade and sweet tea. Those were the go to drinks for places in the south. The crushed ice at the bottom of the barrel soothed them, because it was 100 degrees outside almost every week that summer. Some couldn't take the heat so they stayed inside sending their children to get their plates. And as sad as it was, some were afraid to come out because they didn't want their skin to become darker. The roots of racism were deep and would take some time to come out of.
"Sister Gracie is so pretty, I wonder why she hasn't gone off and got married?" Velma commented, handing off a plate to one of the children.
"Me too." Heidi agreed. Lorraine gave a presumptuous look.

"What's that look for?" "No ma'am." Rainy grunted. She knew how Velma could get second hand gossip out of her.
 "C'mon tell me." She begged.
"Well this is off the record..." she whispered and the girls came in closer.
"I heard Gracie was married once but got that woman's nasty disease because her husband was stepping out on her. Had a mistress on the other side of town."
"I know you are lying." Heidi gasped.
"And I heard she can't have children." She said lastly
Velma shook her head and got back to scooping potato salad.
"Well that really is a shame. She's so beautiful and I know someone who would love her company." Velma suggested.
"Who?" Rainy cocked her eyebrows out of confusion.
"Your man." She joked.
They all giggled while Lorraine rolled her eyes like she always did. "Don't look now but David is on his way for a plate. Bet he's waiting on you to fix him one." They looked.
"Dang I said don't look, could y'all be more obvious?" Heidi asked sarcastically. Before they could get into an argument David and the boys approached the line. But this time there were some new faces in the group. Compliments of little Jimmy Howard.
"Good afternoon ladies."
"Afternoon minister David" Lorraine said inconspicuously.
"Now I told you Rainy, you're more than welcome to call me David. You've been like family."
"Like family?" She questioned half way, smiling.
"Well no not like family m-more like..." he started stumbling. David didn't mean like family in a sense like a sister. He meant she was really close to his family.

"I know what you mean." She teased. "You do?" David sounded relieved.
"Yeah I do. Macaroni cheese?"
"Don't mind if I do."

After David the whole crew got their plates they even got extra hushpuppies. John Ferrari got out of his tent and came for a plate as well.
"Hey guys." "Hey Johnny." The girls said with excitement. "I'm ready to get some of this good cooking and hospitality. See if it'll live up to its hype."
"Well ain't nothing like the southern home grown food honey."
"I bet." Heidi didn't say much to him, not after the encounter they had at the tent ,weeks ago.
He gave her one last look before departing and sitting at the table with the fellas. Her cheeks turned rose red. Velma took notice.
"What's that all about?"
"What?" She answered confused. "You usually have something to say to ole Johnny boy."
"Well not today." Velma suspiciously glared at her.
"I pray to God there ain't no funny business going on little girl. You look at him like I am looking at this piece of cake."
"I didn't know you were my mother, there isn't anything going on. And if there was, it's none of your business." This sharp saying struck Velma in her chest. She had never heard her little sister Heidi speak to her in that way. "Then I guess you've got it all figured out." She softly said leaving the table. Velma was tough on the outside but on the inside she was a soft girl, who just cared for loved ones and wanted to be heard instead of being dismissed. Although they weren't many years apart in

age, in some ways Velma was more advanced. She also had more common sense than Heidi. Heidi was more bright eyed and was open to unusual experiences. Velma was just the opposite. Heidi sighed.

"Velma!" She approached the church stairwell where Velma decided to take a seat. "Ole cry baby." She whispered beneath her breath.

"I heard that." She pointed.

"Look I'm sorry for snapping, I just want you to believe in me sis. And know that I'm not some dumb little girl like I used to be." She explained. Velma looked up. "I don't think you're dumb, I just want you to be careful. Black girls get raped everyday. And if it's by a white man you think they're gonna care? No. They're gonna say you were a jezebel hussy and you seduced him." Heidi knew this was the truth.

"I'm sorry." Heidi voiced. "Do me one favor."

"And what's that?" "Don't

Be sorry, be careful."

Unfortunately David never got around to asking. So when it was 12:30 am and the waters were asleep David climbed out his bed and put on his yellow dress shirt and pleated pants. He jumped out the side of his window landing on the grass by the fence. Jimmy shined his automobile lights. He stayed a couple of nights with the waters so he knew not to wake them. David grabbed the door and climbed in the passenger seat. "Who would have thought that David Waters would be breaking curfew?"

"Shhh man, my pops and ma are asleep."

He warned. "The girls too?" Jimmy asked.

"Yeah, let's get out of here." They said lastly before pulling off and going to the shack.

When they read the sign it said Sam Cooke was a special guest tonight who was going to be singing some of his secular hits. 'Bring it to me' and 'you send me.'

"Can't believe Sammy is singing here, it ain't really classy." David voiced. He was expecting Sam to be on the dick Clark show or at the copacabana although those chances were slim.

"Good." Jimmy exclaimed, now putting his Cuban cigar in his mouth. They opened the revolving door to folks on the dance floor. People were bumping and grinding and doing this new wave called dirty dancing.

Sheryl, a waitress , walked past Jimmy and David as they sat at their tables. David hunched his shoulders looking around. "You want your usual Jimmy?" Sheryl asked.

"Yeah baby doll." He winked. She strutted across the floor taking his order. And then Another girl came to their table. She had light brown skin and dimples. Her hair was black and was loosely curled from the rollers she had used earlier.

"Hey Jimmy." "Hey Dee dee." He said stiffly.

"Aren't you gonna introduce me to your friend?" She looked between David and Jimmy Howard.

He cleared his throat "David this is Miss Dee dee. Dee dee, David." He answered begrudgingly.

David nodded. "How ya doing?"

"Delighted to meet you David. Little Jimmy, where have you been hiding this cutie?" She joked eying David down with a seductive pouty lip. She giggled and took his order for food and drink.

"Well I hope you feel welcomed at sugar ray's juke joint" she said scurrying off with his order.

"Man, who was that?" David asked, his eyebrow raised. "Don't even think about it." his friend warned.

Jimmy sipped on his drink and looked away. Soon the MC gave an introduction to Sam Cooke. He started singing and more people came in along with uninvited tagalongs. David looked and to his surprise Velma was trickling in on the dance floor by accident. She looked like a deer in headlights.

David rushed over, Jimmy behind him.

"What are you doing here?" He questioned.

After people stopped bumping into her she could finally pay attention. "Don't try to turn this on me mama's boy, what are you doing here. I saw you hop in Jimmy's car so I took our uncle's key and followed y'all." She said,

How could she go from looking lost to getting all loud and bold all of a sudden?

"Velma this ain't no place for a lady" David said.

"You aren't wrong." She eyed him, looking around in the joint. "I'm getting a drink." She stormed off.

David gave an exhausting sigh. Jimmy laughed at him. She sat on a stool by the bar. Sipping on some water. That's all she knew. A gentle man sat in a seat beside her. He wasn't really a looker but he had nice clothes and fine hair going for him. "Can I get you something beautiful?" He said grinning initially.

"Uhh no thanks I'm fine." She smiled wearily.

"You sure? I could get you some Hennessy or if you are not that type of lady I can get you a Shirley temple." He chuckled.

"It's fine really." She mouthed "I really don't mind." He insisted.

"She said she's fine." Out of nowhere Jimmy swooped in getting a refill on his drink.

"Hey I didn't mean anything by it man." The gentleman threw his hands up. And walked away from the stool. "I can handle myself, you know." Velma said with her teeth gritted.
"Would it kill you to say thank you sometimes Velma? That guy is a country pimp."
"Pimp?!" She asked in disbelief.
"Pimp." He solemnly answered.
"But he was so nice."
"And that's how they get you."
He proceeded to drink his drink.
"Can I get a Shirley temple for
The lady- "wait I'll have what he's having. Velma boldly interjected.
Jimmy's eyes widened. "You want what I'm having?"
She shook her head yes. "I won't get drunk will I?"
"Baby that's not how it works." He teased me.
She blushed at the afterthought of him calling her baby. "Since you're on my Dime I want to let you have more than a sip, you could be a lightweight. Don't want the reverend to send me to hell." he laughs.
"That's not how it works." She said, wiggling her eyebrows.
"Okay smart a-."
"Ayye watch it now" she joked. Velma has never been one for profanity.
"My fault." When the drink came back she took a sip.
She swallowed and made a face like she had been sucking on a lemon. "I'm guessing you ain't too keen on the drink."
"It's alright, don't see why people act like they gotta have it. "
After you sent me had been playing for a little while the musicians changed up gears.
"Alright band and the gang." Sam Cooke yelled in the mic.

"We're gonna do something a little different tonight. All the fellas grab a lady and sway to this tune." He rhymed. The mic amplifies his sultry voice.
"You ever been in love with someone but you have your ups and downs. And it seems like the shaggy ole girl wants to leave you. Well that's what this song is about. Gang are you ready?!
"Yeah." They replied instantly.
The band played the introduction and Sam sung.

*"If you ever change your mind, about leaving me, leaving me behind. Oh bring it to me bring your sweet loving, bring it on home to me"*

The fellas did just what he requested; they grabbed their partners in for a swing.
Velma sat back in awe looking at everyone. 'So in love' they seemed.

"God, knows I've tried to treat you right
I just stayed out, stayed out all night
Oh, want you to bring it to me
Bring your sweet loving
Bring it on, bring it on, bring it on home to me"
Jimmy got out of his seat moving swiftly to Velma's eyesight. He stuck his hand out.
"Would you like to dance?" She looked at him for a moment and was swayed by his intense charming smile and the eyes that could see through you.

"No thanks." A wave of regret in her voice. She thought Jimmy was gonna take off. But to her surprise he just took off his jacket and sprawled out on the chair next to her
"I'll just sit here with you then." she nodded.
"I mean I can't."

She replied with guilt.
"Of course you can."

Velma knew she was in for a ride when Jimmy gave his infamous smirk. He grabbed her hand pulling her to the dance floor. She stepped forward placing her hand in his hand and her other on his shoulder. Jimmy placed his palm on the middle of her back. Her body was rigid, stiff even. They swayed in sync to the music. Velma was nervous and wanted to bite her nails. She couldn't figure out how she ended up on the dance floor with Jimmy Howard, the very boy she despised. And thought he was a real heathen.

"Hey just relax, don't worry about it." He said. She then relaxed her stance. Jimmy smoothly enclosed himself near her.
"I've never danced before..."
she confessed looking up at him. She expected him to laugh. She was so embarrassed. Growing up in a strict background secular music was scarce. And Velma was too much of a goodie two shoes to
Venture out.

"That's okay, dancing is all about how you feel mama's" he chuckled. Jimmy looked around to make sure others weren't gonna bump into them. He brought Velma in closer and surprisingly she didn't fight back. She guessed this was the way to dance. Jimmy wore a white button down with suspenders and his collar happened to be open. Velma wore her dress from the picnic. It was light blue with white polka dots. Her hair was rolled up into pin curls. She was wearing white petite sandals. And big pearl earrings.It was difficult for her to grasp she never knew when the next step or move was. But Jimmy was almost elegant with every turn. She slowly became comfortable with his lead and it seemed like they got closer and closer. His hand grazed her back and slowly she felt comfortable enough to lay her head against his chest. The music kept going.

Sam was singing his heart out. And the room was so hot that sweat trickled from everyone in the shack.
"Bring it to me, bring it home to me."
"We're gonna do a spin." He whispered. She softly nodded her head. He twirled her around and she landed on his chest with her head facing the other way. He wrapped his arms around her, rocking her from side to side. She could smell his cologne that hadn't worn off and his hitched breathing she could feel on her neck. But they kept swaying.

Velma was no longer stiff. She felt her heart beating rapidly and wasn't sure of what was happening. He turned her around once again and swiftly brought her in with him. This time his forehead touched hers. He eyed her the whole time. And then it transpired, Jimmy brushed his hand swiftly and softly against the back of her bodice, she felt a warm tingling sensation. Not knowing how to respond She felt as if she was losing control. His hand moved past her mid back and lower. She internally gasped. The song ended abruptly. And she could feel the stares from the crowd around them.

Dee dee came up to Jimmy.
"She's a pretty one." She commented.
Velma looked around absent minded scratching her neck.
"Jimmy, who is she?" She further questioned him, but it was clear that was her intent from the beginning.
Velma began to move but Jimmy caught her hand telling her to not leave.
"Dee Dee moves out the way girl." "Oh now I'm a girl that needs to move out the way." She rolled her eyes. Velma sensed some familiarity between the two, feeling uncomfortable she kept walking.

"Jimmy let go of my hand." Velma said solemnly. He had no choice but to let her go.
"Why ?." He reached out to her once again. They were gaining stares from the crowd. People were whispering to each other.
"This is wrong, this is so wrong." She said walking away from him her hands were pushing people out the way. David brushed past her as he saw what had happened.

"What did you do to her man?!"
"nothing , I only asked her to dance." David Jr. looked in disbelief, but he trusted his best friend. He had an inkling but his sister's business was her own. He just prayed it wasn't what he thought it was. Jimmy was his friend and almost like a brother, but he certainly wasn't the marrying type. And he had a long list of women from all over the state he dealt with. Velma wasn't ready for that type of thing.

John really stole the hearts of the people, he convinced reverend waters to let Heidi come along and do interviews. And well, they did them ,the SCLC was coming to town. John saw the hunger in Heidi's eyes for journalism and research. And he made sure that he fed her curiosity, this particular day they decided to have a break and have a nice picnic in the park in Beverdille. All eyes were on them, Heidi would see black families pass by them and John was getting stares from people walking out the pharmacy.

"Mr. Ferrari, you've finally made it to our part of the town." the ginger haired lady says.
"I have, it's nice and quaint. I'm working and having lunch. Would you like to join me and Heidi?"

With disdain, Miss Walker cuts her eyes at Heidi sitting near John.
"I think maybe another time, but it's very kind of you to want to help the less fortunate. If I were you I'd be careful of the company I keep though, John."
With that she turns around with her curls swinging from side to side and her frame joining her.
Emma Walker was basically Beverdille royalty and part of the Walker family legacy. It was clear as day that she thought that John should have been fraternizing with the white part of town and not Heidi and her people. It was also clear that she probably had romantic intentions for him.

Heidi snickers and rolls her eyes. "What is it?" John asked.

"Nothing, nothing at all." she sighs, knowing that her making a big deal about it would only bring attention to the obvious.

John sits back on the tree bark continuing to read the book 'stride toward freedom: montgomery story'
"It's a good book."

"Hmm. " John silently agrees.
"He's literally making history before our eyes. This movement is a new phenomenon at the New York Times." He says while putting the book down.
He fixates his eyes on Heidi, only to find out she's looking at something else.
The water fountains.
The old damage faucet was labeled 'colored'
And the newer shinier one was labeled 'white'

He thought the separate but equal talk was a joke, but coming to North Carolina began to open his eyes .
 "Are you thirsty? Maybe you should go get a sip." He suggested. She turned around to look back at him.
"I'm not, just wondering why our things are beaten down or passed down to us. But we're supposedly separate but equal?" She sighed.

"Exactly, I was thinking the same thing." he agrees.

"Dr. King is gonna bring his movement here and we're so glad to hear his methodology. Well I for one am. I heard about the training for college kids to be nonviolent. In protest against racism and bad treatment." she says.

" You're phenomenal, you know that?" John sits up to look at her rant on. A term of endearment he couldn't find to save his life. She was just otherworldly. He loved how intelligent she was, how carefree she was. He genuinely wondered how someone like her could be this radiant with all life had dealt her with. He could only assume that her religious ties produced this.

"Why do you believe in God?"

"What?" she asked shockingly.
Being on the southern beltline people rarely asked those kinds of questions. Which meant one thing. John wasn't very religious or he was what some people called an atheist.
"I have no logical explanation, I just do. I've been taught about God since I was a little baby. My life doesn't make sense without him somewhere in it."
Heidi explained. It still wasn't enough for him. Sure he could say he was Catholic but that was in name only. Heidi wouldn't call herself the devout one but she was more clear on her theology and could at least explain a few bible stories, if put on the spot.

It was impossible to live with the Reverend waters and not quote the 23rd psalm from memory alone. John just wanted to know did it mean anything? Or was it meaningless.
"Okay." he said. Not wanting to say anything further for the mere fact that she could get offended by his views.
Time had passed and it was almost dinner time at the Water's house. Heidi invited John to come over. Yes it was strange to

have someone of his complexion to dine with them. But the waters were adamant about taking on the movement philosophies. In them were solid christian principles.

He joined them for dinner, and experienced the sweet southern hospitality once more. All of these kind gestures were nice but he wanted to know more about Heidi. And he wanted to be the man to unlock the free spirited version that hid behind her cold brown eyes, they only lit up when they talked about journalism, civil rights, and something he and Heidi were starting to get into, poetry.

That evening after dinner there was still light outside, with daylight savings it was impossible for it to feel like the evening. Heidi took a walk with John to see him off. He took an item out of his back pocket, not used to the southern heat he tied his jacket around his waist.

"Here," he says.

" What is this?" Heidi asked, puzzled.

"Poetry, only the greats." he smiled at her curiosity.

"Remember we read and analyzed some of them," he reminded her.

"Be calm- love me today." she quotes.

"Beethoven." says John.

"These are just love poems John, why? Some are a bit racy." she exclaims.

John laughs

"But they are authentic," he replies. Shaking her head Heidi readies herself to return the book back in John's hand.

"I can't accept these." John grabs Heidi by her waist, looks deeply in her eyes and murmurs,

'Why not?' They both gaze into eachothers eyes. Leaving John no choice but to lean down to kiss her leaving his imprint on her.

It was a wonderful kiss, a trip to paradise.

But it was a forbidden one. When Heidi opened her eyes, she turned really red.

"Why? Why did you have to kiss me? It was good the way it is." she exclaimed.

" Because I wanted to." he jesters. "John, it's not funny." she says her body is almost shaking.

"Did I misread the situation? I thought we were enjoying each other's company. Correct me if I am wrong." John asked bewildered.

Blinded with tears and rage, Heidi grabbed the book and ran back inside the house.

John had no idea the can of worms he had opened.

She fought conflicted feelings about him already, and she dealt with the disapproving ways of her family. They could not fault her for being a little disparate, her genetic make-up was both white and black. Essentially society had forced her to choose. And in that choosing the other decisions made up themselves. Being with a white man was troublesome, and she didn't know if she wanted to fight for the kind of love that would bring more pain and disappointment in her life.

**Chapter 8**

The next day, Ethel took the girls and decided to bring the reverend with her. He didn't get out much these days, the planning for the conference kept him overwhelmed, but in Ethel's persistence she decided to make it a family day. Ethel stopped at her favorite spot in town to pick up a few dresses. But she noticed the sign in the window saying the building was for sale. It wasn't as colorful and elegant as Miss Albertina would have decorated it.

"For sale" Ethel quotes aloud.

"It's gotta be the walker's family doing." David sr. Said after her.
His suspicions were valid though. Beverdille in the past had a few slaveholding families, then after the civil war came the sharecropping, one of the big families in their area was the walkers who brought plots of land years ago. The pharmacy was down the street from the tailor shop. Mr. And Mrs. Walker had been trying to get it off of Albertina's hand for a while. But she'd refused each time. She knew how much weight it carried to be a woman of color owning her own business and building. So what truly happened to make it go on sale? A woman like Albertina was steady and sure. And wouldn't leave at the sight of a little confrontation. The Water's stumbled in noticing her putting the ugly mannequin into a large horizontal bin. As she struggled to stand back up, she looked over at the door hearing their steps."Reverend? What are you doing here?" the reverend, as in much shock as her, realigned his tie that was attached to his collared shirt.

"Well we thought we'd come and visit like we used to and now it looks like you are shutting down." he said, his voice slightly confused.

Albertina looked down defeated.

" I've been meaning to tell you about it Reverend, but you and the first lady have many other important things to worry about then this old shop." she said.

" Don't say that Albertina this shop is a treasure, and every colored woman in town has a place they can shop at and buy their own clothes from,from their own." Ethel said with a meaningful gaze.

Albertina grabbed Ethel's hand and placed the key in it. "Now that I know you feel that way, I know I am making the right choice."

"Albertina." Ethel says, stunned.

"Dear I am 67, my children are grown and my husband Garvey is dead. My daughter Gwendolyn and her family have a place for me to stay, I am getting older… don't try to convince me to stay. Dreams are for you youngins." she laughs.

"But what about the for sale sign in the display case?"

"Oh Heidi and velma, one of yall grab that for me." Heidi obliged and took the sign down, handing it to Albertina.

She took the piece of paper and ripped it up in front of the Waters family. She grinned at all of them.

" Ethel I am making you the new owner of this shop."

"But Al-"

"No excuses, you're one of the best seamstresses in town. Everyone respects you and the Reverend. You would be a lovely businesswoman." It was clear that Albertina had thought about this for some time. She knew the family would be hesitant to take it, but there was no other choice. If she didn't sell it or give it away to someone the choice would be made. Bill Walker, who owns the pharmacy and most of the land around Beverdille would have taken it and turned it into a parlor for some of the whites in town. That was the last thing Albertina wanted. And she was sure nobody favored that decision.

"It's your's, I am moving and taking the train to Chicago in two days." she had sold all of her belongings and left the house she raised her kids in to her next of kin, her mind was made up.

After a day of praying and discussing with David and the kids, Ethel was ready to graciously accept. The truth is she always dreamed of having her own shop. But she didn't want to draw too much attention to herself. It's a shame that good things have to be kept a secret, everyone wouldn't be happy when she started the business. So she and David and the kids devised a plan to keep it under wraps until they knew for sure it was safe.

The bins that Albertina left in the shop were still of good use, she left fabric, sewing machines, pins and scissors. And she left ugly mannequin. Luckily Ethel did not have to start from scratch. The girls decorated the place in their mothers taste. And David Jr along with Jimmy did any heavy lifting with the packages and painting. Just as Ethel was setting up her station the shop's door opened.

"Are you taking any customers today?"

**Chapter 9**

'Conference day'

*" The ultimate measure of a man is not where he stands in moments of comfort and convenience, but where he stands at times of challenge and controversy."-Dr. King*

"You think just because you get along with the negros in the south, you understand our pain?"
She had finally gathered the courage to give John Ferrari a piece of her mind.
"No Heidi, I never said anything like that."
"You didn't have to. The way your acting says it for itself."
"I'm just saying back home my folks are Italian and we came over decades ago with nothing. We get treated badly all the time but that doesn't mean we complain."
"But Johnny you're not getting the part where my people didn't come over here for the mere fact of having a better life. No. We were dragged over here against our will for free labor. Slavery ended 93 years ago. You see, my grandmother is still living."
She walked away to the opposite side of where John was standing. They had been in the church yard preparing for the conference that everyone in town had been waiting on. "Come on now, don't paint me as the bad guy, I'm the good guy. I'm on your side."
"Side?" Her eyes widened and her voice became louder. "Yes I believe in equal rights, it's just why can't y'all pick yourselves up by your own boot straps?"
"Think about it, I know you're capable of recognizing other people's perception."

"That's just it, it's your perception. You shouldn't talk on these issues if you don't know Mr. Ferrari." You could hear a pine cone dropping from the tree. But before John could utter another word Heidi Briskly walked away stepping into the church building.

The Conference was going to be packed. The NAACP wanted reverend waters to host it in the eastern region. Heidi was angry, almost blowing steam out of her nose. She was passionate when it came to her people. Anger may have not been the appropriate word to describe her feelings, down right disgusted was more like it. She never allowed people to escape with ignorance and she certainly wasn't starting with John Ferrari. It didn't matter how complicated her feelings were starting to become for him. She angrily marched past the pews in church, almost bumping into a couple of men in black suits. "Careful sweetheart." A large man said. She looked frail. The two men moved away from each other suddenly and she couldn't believe who she was seeing right now.

She browsed him from his dress shoes to his white buttoned up shirt, to his round face. He was a young man and had butter pecan skin. She just knew he was older by the way he sounded on his speeches but seeing him had proved her wrong. Did her eyes deceive her? She had visited Ebenezer Baptist church plenty of times growing up but seeing him now was so different.
"Well if it isn't the little lady Heidi."

He reached for her to shake hands.

"Dr. Martin Luther king!" He chuckled lightly at her mysticism.
"Yes I know I'm even funnier looking in person right." He answered. He had a clear sense of humor.
"Oh no I'd never think that." She shyly said.
He grinned at her, and patted her shoulder to reassure her, he was only jesting.
"Listen where can I find reverend waters?"
"Umm he's right in the pastor's study, Dr. King."

She pointed in the directions of her uncle's office. She began walking towards it only until the secretary Gracie noticed and got up from her file cabinet. Sister Gracie was about 5'1, with honey brown skin, a silhouette that was almost perfect. Her lips were carefully traced with a bright red lipstick and she wore a baby blue mid length skirt and a white blouse with ruffles, stopping at the top of her arms. It was accompanied with yellow 3 inch pumps. She didn't walk but she graced the hall until she met the ministers and Dr. king. She smiled with Joy upon his arrival. "Martin!" She jumped in his arms as he chuckled. "Grace, my Gracie has grown all up."
He said kissing her on the cheek.
"How is A.D. doing?" She fixed her clothes and patted the little frizzled piece of hair back in place.
"Oh you know him, he's still trying to find his way through school. It's his Last year I suppose."
"Well when you see him tell him ole Gracie asked about him" she lastly said. One of the ministers cleared his throat. "Oh heavens forgive me." She led them inside the Reverend Water's office. They waited shortly til he arrived. Heidi stood in the office watching the ministers discuss what she thought would

be in the meeting. Sister Gracie gave Heidi a bewildered approach. "Pardon us ministers, we will leave you to attend to the important matters." The look on Heidi's face was unbelievable. She didn't want to leave the office. She was getting an inside peek into what was going on.

Gracie slightly pushed her out the door.

"Sister Gracie!" She whined. "Come on girl, folks are starting to come in." And sure enough she was right. People gathered to sit in the pews.

The meeting attendance was monstrous.

They both went their separate ways. Heidi went to the conference table and started checking to see if those who signed up paid their dues. And many people claimed they had but names weren't there. She couldn't throw them out so she didn't say anything. Gracie didn't either.

She looked further down the list and saw a name that read "Stephen Jackson." She heard a voice say. She looked up and there he was. He was a busboy at one the most famous restaurants in Beverdille, and the most sought out musician in the region. He had a Lazy grin proceeding to hold out his hand towards her. She shook it.

"Am I... am I good to go?" He inquired. "Of course."

Heidi smiled back pointing to an empty seat.

As many people passed through she found herself appreciating the young man's handsome qualities. Qualities she looked at since their days in high school.He noticed and gave her a warm smile in return.

After finishing registering people, she got up to get a drink of water. Turning around she metaphorically bumped into Ferrari.

"Hey." "Greetings, Mr. Ferrari." "Greetings? Since when did we become so formal?" He asked, confused.

"Is there anything I can do for you sir?" Heidi looked away and she even offered him a cup of water.

"Heidi, come on don't be mad at me." "Is there anything I can do for you Mr. Ferrari?" She asked once again.

"I just want to talk." "Whatever do you mean? She answered mockingly. Heidi overlooked John and went on to serve the next guest in the conference line. She whispered looking around.

"I get it, you're scared but I know I feel something and I have a feeling it's not just one sided." He tried grabbing her hands but she carefully and swiftly removed them.

"I look forward to seeing your story in the paper." He cursed under his breath. And She turned on her heels walking away. Heidi saw that Stephen stood up to offer a seat. Stephen looked across the room to see what the commotion was about. "Hey are you alright?" "I'm fine." All John could do was look. He knew that she was going to make it hard for him. She wasn't an easy fish to catch, or an easy woman to impress. Heidi was the least impressionable person he met but the most eye-catching of them all. The one that made his heart skip a beat, he had to have a sip of what she was giving. He suspected she was trying to make him jealous. And if he had to play the game to get her then he'd enjoy it. 'Okay Miss Heidi Jamison' he thought. "I'll play your game, not playing to lose." he whispered under his breath and began to take photos.

**Chapter 9**

Dr. King delivered a brilliant speech about hope, dedication, and peace and love. He stood on the mount of the Church of Christ temple, gaining the attention of the 500 people sitting in the building. They were enamored by his grace and how he spoke so eloquently yet so passionately. This man's words could ignite and unite a whole group of people to fight for something. They saw what he did with the Boycott in Alabama. How he supported the mother of civil rights, Rosa Parks. All of the coloreds in that region worked together and got a law that was unfairly removed. But that was only the beginning.

Reverend Waters sat in the pulpit sporting a black fancy collared shirt. He also wore a pocket chain along with it. He was seated beside the SCLS. the assistant minister Vixen was nowhere to be found. He was more than likely mad that he couldn't be on the board of hospitality; he wanted the chance of speaking to Dr. King just like the others. But they were on a tight schedule. And although the Reverend called on favors, he still treated this opportunity like a privilege. 'Don't talk the reverend king's head off' he'd warned. No one took heed of the warning. Folks came from various parts of North Carolina, wanting to meet the man himself. He walked with such humility and a warm smile. It felt welcoming even to the most estranged fellow in the midst. There was not one person that he couldn't work his magic on and they too would instantly feel like they could make a difference in the movement. "...if a man hasn't discovered something he would die for, he isn't fit to live." He spoke on the microphone. His voice roared across the building. He wanted the people to come together and march. He wanted people to promise to support the surrounding black businesses. "If we cannot eat or shop at these various places with our white brothers and sisters, then they don't deserve our hard earned money." Heidi sat near the front but she couldn't help it, she checked her surroundings seeing the undeniable support of the people. "Amen, brother!" a young man agreed. She thought about how it would be if her parents were alive and came to this gathering. They were activists in their own right. It only made sense for her to follow the same path. The plan to boycott in North Carolina was audacious. They would refuse to take county bus lines. Refuse to eat at the local shops and if they couldn't use the restrooms at the gas station store house then those folks just wouldn't get the money.

"Stephen Jackson huh?" "That is my name." he grinned. He grabbed his case and put the alto saxophone that swung over his neck into the case.
"What were you doing at this conference, don't you have somewhere to play?" Heidi playfully asked." well if you must know Dr. King was in town and I think it's safe to say that many colored folks would shut down where they're at to come to see him." Dr. King was a beacon of hope and a mouthpiece for the black struggle. So naturally anyone who cared about their community wanted to hear what he had to say. They walked past the church exterior bumping into clergy members and King's staff. But then he passed some local musicians who were having a discussion. "Hey, Stephen, come over here."

Heidi invited her siblings And Lorraine to come to the shack. Stephen was apparently playing that night at the joint. She needed to escape from feeling different from everyone, for just one moment. And if Stephen Jackson could provide it, who was she to turn it down? Stephen was the talk of the town, a star quarterback and a mathematician. But he just couldn't stay in school, desperate times caused desperate measures. So he traded in his diploma and ball throwing speed for a nice suit and a saxophone. Although God given, his charming smile too. That night after the conference was one of those special times when people talked about how you had to be there.

And for the water's sake maybe that wasn't all together true. Heidi watched Stephen play the whole night, he gathered the attention of listeners. There was nothing like music, secular or holy; that could bring black people together. The walls were sweating, the ceiling caving in. The shack, Sugar Rays, was no place that was considered up to the county's code. Though the owner

Had their ways of getting around the codes and the law. The owner bribed them with promises of eternal booze.

As the night progressed the band had simmered down and the crowd eventually began to thin out. All smiles and cheers, the gang went to congratulate Stephen Jackson. He was surprised to see the Pastor's kids coming to support him.

"Yall have to leave, Reverend Waters isn't gonna preach on me." he joked.

"You're living in sin! Come out of the darkness, backslider!" he mocked.

"That's Daddy alright." David Jr. agreed. Being as light hearted as possible, but it was the truth. The gang had a few more drinks and circled around the table. The band played a few more moments until things got interrupted.

A Large burly man, brunette with white streaks of hair appeared in the shack holding a dispatcher and a sheriff uniform. Jerry walker. People were fearful of him because he wasn' a nice man, but then again nobody was in the Walker

dynasty. He looked like his brother Bill, only a bit more husky and less friendly looking. He spit the cigar out his mouth, dusting it off on the ashtray near the bar.
"We should leave." Velma whispered to all of the kids.
David Jr. and Heidi hindered her from any sudden movements. They tried to calm her down and they didn't want their reasonable anxiety to spiral out of hand.
Stephen placed his saxophone down in Heidi's lap, and asked her if she could hold it down for him.
"I'm going to the out house… ladies, gentlemen. I'll be back." he tipped his hat off to the girls that were sitting at the table.
"Let me get a beer, don't hold out on it either." said the sheriff. He adjusted his belt and sat down in one of the seats. While the bartender was making his drink he asked questions about where the owner was, and about how much the juke joint was making each night. He couldn't have possibly known that all records like that were sealed shut. No successful business person and colored person would reveal all of their secrets. Beverdille wasn't Wall Street , but ownership was becoming important these days.
" Tell Frankie, I'm here." The bartender obeyed Jerry once again and grabbed the owner Frankie from the kitchen.

Holding a mop in his hand and cigarette behind his ear, he was surprised to see the sheriff. Still he remained cool.
" To what do I owe this pleasure, Sheriff Walker?"
Smirking, the sheriff took a sip of the drink.
"What is with the formalities Frank, You know you call me Jerry,we're pals." he replied.

Everyone that was left in the shack watched carefully including the Water kids. Jerry Walker presented a sinister aura, any discerning eye could tell he was up to no good.

" Jerry, You told me pay wouldn't be due til the 15th."

"I did say that hmm." he pondered mockingly.
"I figured it wouldn't hurt to collect early since there was a big conference on your side of town. With that *nigger* King disrupting our town, I'm sure business is booming."

Frankie the owner, gulped out of fear and discontent. Looking down he says
"Jerry, I don't have the money. We've been spending it on all the extra booze you and the fellas at the station demanded. The deal we made was the 15th. I'll have it to you by then."

After that Jerry grabbed the bottle from the table, he drank the rest of the alcohol that was left. Frankie made eye contact with the bartender, nodding his head.

Staggering towards the dance floor and dining tables, Jerry started to fidget with his dispatcher and gun in his hand. When he walked closer he squinted his eyes at the gang.

"You." he pointed. David Jr. pointed at himself.
"Get up," The sheriff demanded. David looked at his sisters one last time before obeying the men.

Heidi let a tear slip out her eyes. And cursed under her breath. She wasn't exactly being the brave warrior she thought she could be at this moment.

"Your'e David's boy, ain't ya?"
"Yes sir, I am."
"I can tell. All of you are his youngins. Got no business down here. You're pappy is a good boy, except for when he hosted that King at his church. But I forgive him cause I know it doesn't mean anything. Just a bunch of people complaining." he chuckled in his buzzed state.
"Father." Velma said softly under her breath.
"What do you say, gal? Speak up."

"Father, you called him pappy. That's when you don't know who the father is or who the children belong to. But he's our father… sir." trying hard to not be overly defiant, Jimmy squeezed Velma's hand under the table. He examined her, and whispered
"Stay calm."

"Mmm definitely uppity, but you, holding the saxophone. You're a pretty one." the sheriff did the imaginable and started to whisper in Heidi's ear. Twirling her curls in his hand. She gritted her teeth angrily, and her tears continued to scuttle down her cheek. It was not long before Stephen came back from using the out house.
He hurried along to find his friends in an uncomfortable place.

Silently he assumed his position beside Heidi. He kept eyeing his belongings that she held in her lap. But he didn't wanna further disturb or bring attention to himself.

"I want you to play boy." He directed his attention to Stephen. And Stephen nodded his head.

Stephen picked up his saxophone and hesitantly slung the rope that was attached to his instrument around his neck and the underpart of his shoulder.

He blew a few notes, and it seemed like those few moments were all calm and right. But still there was an eerie silence in the room.

A few minutes later into Stephen's impromptu performance, several footsteps struck the wooden pavement floor. They all looked up and saw a policeman spreading across the shack, with Billy clubs.

The bartender took out his gun from underneath the bar shelf. Cocking back his gun he cut his eyes at the owner. The owner prepared his switchblade. And the Water's kids and the gang are encircled by the law enforcement.

Jerry finally grabs a chair after staggering and laughing for a while. He pulls it adjacent to the kids. He grabs another cigar and lights it up.

The light flickers from a lighter canister.

"Freddie, I am the law and I got the law with me to back me up. Where is the money for

This place. We can report your not up to code and shut this God forbidden hole of a place now." He threatens.

"You said the 15th." Frankie said standing obstinate. When Stephen heard this he grabbed Heidi's hand and whispered.

"Let's go."
"I can't leave my siblings." She mouthed with a complexion of worry.
Stephen understood and then encouraged everyone to get up and start leaving while attention was on the owner and bartender.
So they all grabbed their belongings and followed him out towards the outhouse behind the shack and into the woods.
But for all their efforts, it went to dust when something tragic happened.
Their eyes barely registered the flicker of light before the sound struck like a slap. The noise shocked them and became overwhelming. The burning smell of powder wafted through the air. After everything their ears rung with a distinct echo.

Heidi turned her head swiftly to see that the bullet impaled and targeted Stephen's chest.
The blood was splattered all over her dress because she was holding his hand after all.

And then it happened she let out a deafening screech that all could apprehend.
David Jr. and Jamie ran to her side.

And Velma, stood there. She couldn't say anything and she couldn't offer her sister any hope or word of encouragement. Watching everything that was happening, become benumbing. She was so quiet that Jimmy had to come back to grab her.

As they departed from the woods and carried the body of Stephen into the car with all of his spillage, they could smell

the shack being set ablaze and the screams of the crowd that was left there, shattered glass being thrown everywhere and complete disaster.
They certainly couldn't turn back.


David Jr. sighed, standing in his parents parking lot at 3:49 in the morning, was not the custom. And was a sure way to get rebuked. Although he had the slightest feeling they were up. Growing up his parents just seem to instantly know things.
He rung the doorbell as Jimmy tried to carry Stephen to the car. It was extremely hard to focus as Heidi was still screaming on the ride over from the initial shock.
He prayed that his mom would come to the door instead of his father. The tongue lashing would not be as severe with her. But to his demise his father opened the door, in a white wife beater and a robe with slippers.

The Reverend placed his glasses on his face. He wasn't tired, he looked like he had been up all night and into the early morning.
"Daddy, something awful happened." David Jr. let out.
Senior just extended the door open and let him in, it wasn't long before Jimmy brought Stephen in and grabbed Heidi too. Lady Ethel was waiting by the stairwell and grabbed the girl's arm immediately taking her to the kitchen.
"Where is Velma?" she asked.
"She's in the car mama. But she hasn't said anything." immediately Ethel knew what he was talking about. She wrapped herself in a sheer robe, put slippers on and ran outside to get Velma to come in with her.

She found Velma staring at the windshield and fiddling with her hands.

"Velma? Baby?" Velma heard her and looked into her direction.

"Come with me, it's gonna be okay. You are gonna help me now. Take your sister upstairs, wash her clothes and get her in the tub. And mama will do the rest, okay?"

Velma solemnly nods her head and gazes at her mother.

The house got into emergency mode, and soon the guilt that David Jr felt or the punishment he felt faded. It seemed like his parents weren't trying to preach right now but make the situation better.

David sr. made a call to the house doctor in town, Dr. Mccullough and then he asked the boys if Stephen had any family there.

"He's sister Jackson's boy."

"Sister Jackson is a hard working woman, let's not worry about her until later this morning. I'd hate to be resting and wake up to this kind of news."

Stephen was breathing on his own for quite a while but he was unconscious, Dr. Mccullough watched over him during the day and the boy's mother came over to the house. He fought a good fight but his life was plundered and he simply lost too much blood.

Sister Jackson got to him in time to hear his last words, she was devastated. And cried in the arms of the reverend.

The day of the funeral was surreal, many of Stephen's musician friends came, and several civil right activists came to show their support and solidarity. Though Dr. King didn't give the eulogy; he backed up the reverend and felt it was important to allow him to tend to his flock.

When the musical selections had passed and everyone that had been asked to give remarks gave them, Reverend Waters approached the podium in his all-black robe and white collar. "Saints of God, it's with my deepest regret, that today we are laying to rest another young person. Not just any one though, but one of our young people. I am not one to hold my tongue on the things of God. but one thing I do remember is that brother Stephen was real, he didn't play about the possibility of coming to the Lord. He served our community and was an inspiration to the youth in Beverdille. We baptized him in this church, and I am confident that he knew the savior. It's not my job to talk about what he did away from home or the displeasure at his traveling with maybe the secular artist. But it is my job to preach Jesus and him crucified. One thing we can learn from brother Stephen, is to always come back home. In Luke 15 Jesus decides to share a parable with his followers. The son asks his father for his portion of the inheritance. Sometimes as people we ask God for things too early, we believe we are ready for it."
He pauses to take his breath, and make eye contact with Ethel in the pews. The congregation is packed with people wearing all variations of black, as if it wasn't smoldering outside they wear layered clothing. The women fan themselves, just to feel a bit of coolness.
Looking into her eyes gives him a sense of comfort and a push to keep trucking along.

"The son was eager to get out there. In a sense he had the right mindset, he could ask for anything. Like any parent, even though we feel our children aren't ready for something, we love them and want to see them happy. So the father gave the son his inheritance. The son went away and had the time of his life then he squandered it recklessly. While the father has another son that stayed home. I am not here to condemn either party. We preachers get it wrong and rebuke the person who may have asked for the inheritance and we praise the one who stays. But don't you know that you can be present in a situation but still be a backslider in your heart?"

"Amen!" the congregation exclaimed.
"Let me tell you something, the Father represents God in this text, when the son took his riches and spent it partying, drinking and buying materialistic things, he had a good time. But he also lost himself in chasing that lifestyle, he got to a place where he felt like he couldn't come back. At least not as his son.
But I'm here to tell you, that nothing you do can separate you from the love of God. I'm here to proclaim the word of the Lord, that you can come back home." The reverend started getting excited in his sermon. He cured his brother Julius to start playing the organ.
"Hey, you can run to your father's house, and your father can run to you. I don't care what you've done, why you've done it, or who you've done it with." the Reverend tuned up his voice speaking in a rhythmic flow. The congregation became enamored with his delivery and message.
"If you are the son that went away or the one that stayed there is room at the cross, Stephen is not here anymore, I can't

preach to Stephen anymore. But all I know is he heard the gospel, and he made his choice. Oh children, the father loves you ,even if you are in a back sliding condition."

"Come on back, you backslider. Come to Jesus, he's got you." Sitting in the congregation all of the water kids shed tears. The pandemonium that took place in the church was indescribable. Reverend Waters had truly preached an uplifting message, so much that the congregation had an emotional reaction. Some people cried, some people lifted their hands, and others were even emboldened to dance.

Throughout that season the church lost many members and ministers. But the one thing no one could take from the Reverend was his anointing and gift to encourage people during low times.

The sermon at Stephen's funeral acknowledged the condition of the backslider. David Jr
Heidi, and Velma didn't know that their fathers word would be something that stayed with them, throughout their life.

After the funeral, things drastically changed. Life as they know it became something they wish they could get away from. If there was an escape clause that would be great.

The Summer with the Waters had been significant, but they faced many evasive challenges. In their faith and in their family. They elevated in social status as well as wealth and with status came influence; better yet clout. Dr. King became a family friend and any time he gave speeches in the carolina's he needn't fret because the Waters had a home for him. Since the Boycotts caught a lot of attention from business men and the government, it caused him trouble.

He received death threats and got bricks thrown at his house and the Cadillac that he'd be seen riding in with the other fellow ministers. But it was nice that other fellow blacks like the waters had his well being in mind.

## Chapter 10
### The backsliders

**1961**

" Goodness gracious." Velma heaped as she tossed a third pair of trousers across the bedroom floor. She kept speculating about her figure in the long body mirror. She sighed feeling hopeless.
"I just went up another dress size, mom will kill me." frowning at her waist line and bottom half she turned around to find Heidi, reading a book.
She cleared her throat and as if on que Heidi looked up.

" Once again Velma, you're overreacting, you look good."

" I've gone up 3 dress sizes, girl I look like a pillsbury can." Heidi couldn't contain her laughter. She knew Velma had been conscious about her weight and size since their childhood. Velma was always on the fluffy side and when she turned about 13 her mother put her on a strict military diet. It pained velma but if she was going to enter the society ball for her 14th birthday she had to make changes. Life wasn't always fair to her, Heidi had guessed that was the reason why she was as poised as she was but still a little rough around the edges.

As time progressed Velma just threw on a button up along with a high waisted printed pencil skirt.

Still at night Heidi asked " you're going to see him?"
"See who?" she replies.
Heidi sucks her teeth.
As if no person could see through her guise.
"Oh. Jimmy. I mean I suppose so. He hasn't written to me in a year and he's now stationed at Fort bragg."

"Does he know?" Velma twisted her ring around her third finger. She didn't know how it happened so fast but she was engaged to be married by the end of spring. Carter Evers was a relative of the great Medgar Evars. He was a young up and coming minister and after the conference he and Velma had made a connection. The kind one wasn't so sure.

"I think you should tell him. I mean, I know he didn't necessarily profess his love to you. But he's been sweet on you ever since that day you told him off for throwing a football at DJ's head that one summer."
Heidi wasn't wrong at all. But the chemistry between the two wasn't one sided. When Velma was around Jimmy she felt like she was alway on an adventure escaping from her responsibilities. He showed her how to breathe again. And when she was with him there was no pressure to perform. Velma wasn't a water kid, a church girl, a missionary, she was just herself and Jimmy saw that.
Longing for a change of subject , Velma simply asked "Did DJ call yet?... say when he is coming?"

"Daddy said he called last night saying he was finished touring and was gonna hop on the next train to Carolina." she presumed. As Heidi put the last clothespin up in the closet she sat down almost flailing in a prostrate position.

"Home sweet home." she murmured in the covers.

Once the decade changed, one could say it wasn't the same as it was. But even the world was changing. Civil rights laws were finally being passed. The talk of integrating public schools was becoming a thing. And a little building in Detroit ,Michigan was turning the world upside down.
Hitsville USA Motown

"Smokey, this ain't cutting it. It's missing something. The bass line isn't strong enough. Otis is flat and the lead is floating everywhere." David sat in the booth with a pen and paper as he watched the man himself chew out the miracle man.

The truth was the song didn't give that gut feeling. At Motown with Mr. Gordy if you weren't thinking of spending the last dime when they could spend it on a meal. The main question was: was it worth it?
"What's our saying?" Gordy questioned.
"Only hits." Everyone jumped in to answer in the studio. David gritted his teeth out of prevention. He wanted so badly to give a suggestion. But he was just another musician in their eyes, that they could easily replace.
But his hesitation changed to boldness. He raised his hand, gaining attention from both Smokey and Gordy.
"Preacher boy, you got something?"

"Yeah… I do. I was gonna suggest that we take it to church. You know, fill in the baseline, pick up the beat, let the lead singer play around a little bit?"

The room became so silent, one would think you could hear everyone's thoughts.

"I like you." Mr. Gordy said, chuckling and patting David's back.

"Alright, let's take it to church!" Smokey presumed.

After a long studio session David racked up his things and hopped in the back trunk with some of the musicians. Touring was agreeable, but the truth was he missed home. There was nothing like a bed made with clean, soft linen sheets. The smell of Fried chicken in the air and corn fritters on Sunday morning. Or Reverend waters being his personal alarm to get up for service. He missed arguing with Heidi and Velma over bathroom space. He especially craved seeing Rainy's alluring smile on Sunday's.

But about that he didn't know how long he could keep her waiting. Lorraine was an honest woman. Bright with a pleasing personality and a feature to match with it. David since then had moved on with life, she was his dream girl and he wished she knew that. But he could never get his lips to move and let her know that. 'How cowardice' he thought to himself.

**Fort Bragg**

Saying his prayer of gratitude Jimmy sat down on a chair taking his canteen and flogging it down his throat. His feet were sore from a tedious journey. He had been deployed for the last 9 months. And Although he was thankful for the opportunity to make money. He really felt like a number.

Jimmy surprised himself and his unit, he was the most disciplined and most achieved. Even won himself a few medals. Distinguished as all get out and a picture of a gentleman. Anybody in Beverdille wouldn't even be able to recognize him or bet that it was him.
 A few of his friends from the squad started to shriek his name as bent down to fill his canteen with water from the colored water fountain.
"James- James" 3 of them exclaimed.
He rushed his head around, wondering what the commotion was about.
It was inevitable that he would see the 5'2 brown sugar beauty standing approximately 15 ft away from the entry gates.

"Maybe if I started calling you James you'd answer faster." she smiled
Grinning from ear to ear, he grabbed Velma entirely too tight, but she missed him so much she didn't care that he did.
It was the fact that he was there. She prayed many nights that he was okay and living. Her hope deterred when she stopped hearing from him frequently.
"Come here Sweet Cakes"
He hugged her to the fullest and kissed her forehead and all over cheeks. He wanted to peck her lips but his guilty conscience couldn't rest.
When he put Velma down and she came back to her earthly senses she was enveloped by the scent of his manly cologne.
"I'm hungry, are you?"

"I could grab a bite of something." Velma replied.

He took her to the faithful burger shack in the city. As popular as it had been they only had a ten minute wait. It was one of the first burger joints to serve coloreds. Jimmy especially had the favor of being a service man.

As they were seated, Jimmy grabbed her jacket from her shoulders carefully placing it around the chair. They ordered something quickly and began to talk about Jimmy's long adventures.

"You see, this is my airborne pendant. I'm one of the only colored soldiers to get into the training. I've actually been promoted to E-5 this year. I planned an ambush and my sergeant was very pleased with the assessment. He finished as Velma dug through her french fries.

" I'm sorry, is E-5 some kind of classification?"

"That's' exactly what it is." he chuckles, sipping on his Cocola. Jimmy sneakily reaches over velma's plate to grab a fry. But it isn't long before she rebukes him.

" don't dig in my plate."

He winced as she pop's his hand as if he was a toddler taking a cookie out of a cookie jar.

"Dang girl, you need to enlist," he jokes.

Velma was happy to have Jimmy back on the home front. But somehow she sensed he was much different from the one she grew up with, and definitely not little Jimmy anymore. He was a grown man with responsibilities and rank. He's been half way across the world. Jimmy had the reputation of being a maverick in town, but he was no different than other young men, he was just unapologetic about who he was.

When all the formalities were done and the light teasing had passed on Jimmy had to ask her one thing. "How are you? Like For real, how have you been?"

Looking down at her empty plate with ketchup traces, she mouths.

"I'm doing okay. I got a really nice teaching job, I helped mama down at the shop with her tailor shop. You Know help Daddy Waters with the church, even took up some protesting."

"I heard about that, read that in the newspaper. Y'all were doing damage in the city. I don't think I could be non-violent though."

"Well why not? Dr. King said it's a sure thing. Non- violence is the only way. Daddy says it's the most christian thing to do at this point." Velma reports.

" You do know everything your daddy says ain't gold right?"

"Excuse me?'

" I'm not saying your daddy doesn't have a point. I love Reverend Waters as if he was my own father. He's done alot for me and treated me like I was one of his. So don't get me wrong. But if y'all think a bunch of hymns and carrying a pickett is gonna stop the white man from doing what they want to do to us. Yall need to wake up." he said putting his fork down.

" Well, I don't see you trying to do anything to help solve these problems. Let alone sweep the kitchen floor to help aid this movement" She utters.

"Now you just had a little edge in your tone Velma." rolling her eyes Velma spews

" I wouldn't if you weren't being so critical about our people trying to do some good. It may not be so grand according to your standards, Lieutenant Howard but it's something."
He smirked at her, calling him by his title.
They had their arguments and little heated debates every once in a while and they may have played games as kids, but one thing was for sure their passion and intentions for one another was there.
 Had Velma not cared about Jimmy she wouldn't have bothered biting his head off about certain things. One thing, one thing he was curious about
Were they gonna continue to tip toe round their feelings. What's not said didn't need to be because it was understood. Oh yes, immensely understood that every time they came around each other Jimmy would get that old good feeling back. And Velma could look in his eyes and feel like a charmed school girl all the time. It never failed but the games were getting old, she wasn't 19 anymore she needed something substantial.
Substantial like a ring.

" Anyways there's something I've meant to tell you." she proceeds to say with a nervous look on her face.
"Are you okay?"
With a grim expression she takes the ring she had been hiding in her mini purse. She lays it on the table right before his eyes.

They sit in silence and with every passing second Jimmy bores his eyes into Velma's.

"You pulled out a ring?... What does this mean? I mean are you trying to say something to me." he casually sits back in the restaurant chair.

" Carter Evers asked me to marry him." she says.

He bends his head down grabbing a toothpick from the table near the condiments. Playing with the plastic wrapper he replies, " and are you going to marry him?" an honest question for an honest confession. But Velma couldn't help but be annoyed with his calmness. 'If he cared at all, surely he would make a hasty declaration of his love for her and demand she give the ring back.' she thought. But that was dramatic and she knew it.

"I've given thought to it, but I wanted to be fair to you and tell you. He's a good man, he loves God, He's a established minister in the Southern christian leadership conference and he-"

"So that's what it's about. He's a minister, he carries a bible around and wears a white collar around his neck so tight he can't even breathe."
"Now Jimmy I'm not even finished. Anyways he's going to be a great husband one day and I feel like I should marry him but there has been something keeping me at bay and I don't know exactly what." She finishes. Looking at him for clarity.

" I don't either. And I don't even know why you told me. It's not like we even courted. You've been too busy trying to please your'e mommy and daddy. Too scared to even go for what you really want."

He did it again. He had Velma water's loss for words.
" Baby, I ain't trying to hurt you but we got to be real here. We've danced around a relationship for years. I've been wanting you since I don't know when. But I think I may be too out there for you with my non-christian ways and all." it didn't have to be this way at all. Jimmy could change the outcome of the situation but he had a problem of his own. He knew Velma was sweet on him and he was too. The letters and phone calls between them were proof of that. But when times got rough he leaned on others and he knew velma couldn't be there for him the way he needed. He was a grown man with fervent needs about things Velma had no point or reference to. Respecting her wishes and beliefs he had to move on and be realistic.

"You always throw being a christian in my face like it's been such a horrible thing.And I get it you think it's a bunch of rules and people telling you what you can and can not do on God's green earth. And I'm sorry if I gave you that impression. But Jimmy, it's so much more than that. I love being a christian and I want a husband, I want to do things the right way, God's way.

" And I just can't be that for you." he silently murmured.
At first Velma didn't say anything but then she could hear her heart beating. It was as if he made the decision for her and already sent her packing down the altar into the arms of a man she didn't love. Maybe she could learn to love him but it wasn't

the same. She didn't feel a rush or a thrill with him the way she felt with Jimmy.

An adrenaline junkie she may have been. But who could really blame her. She didn't feel like she had much of a life outside of church, work and volunteering for the movement. But she had Jimy and she never knew he could bust her heart with declarations of not being able to change.

"I don't love you for what you can give me. I just do." a lonely tear began to run down the side of her cheek and she grabbed her napkin and went to the nearest restroom.

Cursing under his breath Jimmy balled up his fist. Why did he have to hurt her like that?

Heidi

This year had been tremendously different for Heidi, she was much freer than she had been in the past. In the south everything was traditional and she was seen as being the weird girl. Weird because she didn't chase after boys or the golden marriage ticket. She didn't even think of the finer life. Heidi typically stayed to herself and her studies. But when she moved to New York that all changed. The curly headed Sue began to wear her hair straightened and decided to take her sister's advice on wearing rouge lipstick that made her lips protrude. She found herself wearing a lot of black to cover up the coffee stains she would have endured with all the bright colors. Journalism school had become the peak of her interest, and also interning for the New York times under John Ferarri.

Another complicated situation they were in. Heidi was very Flippant about her decision to deal with him. Heidi didn't have a boyfriend. She had boyfriends and company on saturday evenings.

Ethel would be horrified if she really witnessed how free she had been living.

The New York Times took on Heidi because they believed her perspective was needed. She dealt with alot of prejudice and sneering white press. But she took it as a stamp of approval to keep doing what she needed to do. As time passed she realized in some ways the northern states were just as prejudiced as being down south and that's when she took the train for the heck of it.

John knocked on her door expecting for the mocha skinned woman with wild spirals for hair and reading glasses to open up and let him in for a chinese surprise dinner. As they often did on deadline weeks.

Instead he found a note.

'Dearest John,

Please don't be angry. I just miss my family right now. My Dad has been sick and my mom has been taking care of him and trying to keep up with the tailor shop. Velma has been home holding things down for a while. She is getting married and she needs me. I'll be back as soon as I can.

Yours truly,

Heidi Waters'

It was selfish of him to want to keep her to himself but he wanted her home with him and the puppy they shared. Heidi did things her way and on her own terms. He didn't mind that she saw other people because he knew he couldn't always give her what she needed. But he knew one day that would all stop and she wouldn't run away because their love transcended the color line.

## Chapter 11
## Family matters

Anyone who was somebody envied the waters family. Reverend and Ethel raise their children under dire circumstances and start reaping the benefits of pouring into the kids at their early stages. So why couldn't people see the hard work that was done? They only saw favor and how things were turning out to be. Well with the big church, and community support, the nice home and their educated talented kids who seemed almost too perfect. They couldn't show a moment of weakness because even though people admired them, it was still too good to be true.

"Thank you Dr. Mccullough." Velma said as she placed her fathers jug of water near the table by her parents' comforter.
"It's no problem at all. The reverend is a good man and he married my niece to one of the finest colored professionals a few years back. I owe it to take care of him now. We have to look out for each other, you know?" the tall yellow complexioned man commented. The doctor smiled at Velma and grabbed David Waters hand, giving a cheeky expression. Dr. Mccullough was one of the few black men who was among other healthcare professionals. He went to Shaw University in the olden days and then Leonard Medical school to become a certified physician. It was a wonder he was able to get to Beverdille on short notice.


"You are good to your father." Speaking in third person, David catches his first born's attention while she shuts the door after Mccullough leaves.

"Oh daddy hush you know it's our duty to make sure you're good. I just hate seeing you so helpless."
David laughs sheepishly.
"I'm not helpless. See I've got my newspaper and my bible. And this bell if I need anything."
He picks up the bell and shakes it tirelessly.

"That you do. Do you need anything else before I head out?"

"No, you need to leave. Someone has dress shopping and tailoring to get to." As if she wanted to be reminded of the one thing she had to do.

"I'll see you later daddy."

**Ethel's Tailor shop**

Ethel's tailor shop was starting to show promise in the town. She was one of the best seamstresses there is. Women both black and white stopped by to get alterations and look at the well displayed hats along with dresses. Velma had ordered a dress from designer willie otey kay. She was a
fashionable genius that made elegant garments for young women at their society balls, and then their special days.

"Velma, are you sure you haven't been stress eating? It seems like you've put on a few. We altered this dress 3 months ago and it was perfect."

"Mother. You are saying?"

"You are still beautiful dear, I am just saying you may have put on a little but it's no big deal."

Ethel assured. When it became too silent she wondered for a moment.
"But should I be worried?"
"You can't be suggesting that I'm pregnant."
"Shhh, I'm only asking questions that I should be asking. Why you're a full grown woman and these things happen? I expect minister Evers to be a man of honor but sometimes man can't control their urges"
Astonished by her mother's unbiased approach, she responded with timidity.
"I'm not mom, I thought I was though."
This was a sobering sentence.
But Ethel remained untethered. Her baby girl was a grown woman and her life was beginning.
"Okay." shortly after she asked her to lift her arms to continue alternating her dress.

James would never forgive her if he knew what happened. She doesn't even forgive herself. But she was marrying Carter Evers now. A good honorable guy who hadn't even tried to kiss her yet. Except for when he kissed her forehead when they came back from the movies. Or when he invited her over for his family's thanksgiving. He held her hands under the table. Carter was the most sincere young man she's met. She didn't dislike him.
In fact she enjoyed his company. He was great for her,

"I hate the fact you're going to be a christmas bride."
Heidi said stuffing her face with a walnut from her moms glass dish near the kitchen table.

" You don't even care for weddings. Why are you so opinionated about them now?" Velma chuckled.
"Fair point." she said moving to the christmas apples. Her Daddies health scare sent her packing back to Beverdille and leaving the New York times office. She was forced to be reckoned with in journalism. But this Christmas season she just needed to see her family.

Her impressionable white boyfriend wouldn't understand that because the life he made for them seemed to be accommodating. She loved him but he couldn't replace all those years of staying out late on summer nights with the water kids and Lorraine and the Howard boys. Or skinny dipping at the lake 5 miles down the road. Or the taste of fresh lemonade and selling it for 15 cents.
In New york everything was over priced, over glamourized even. Pouring hot coffee from the stove, Ethel walked past her girls in her house dress with her raven black hair cascading past her back. She would credit her warm red undertone and high classical cheekbones to her Northampton county family ascendants. But that impending southern accent of hers was nothing but her being a resident in Texas for many years.

"Chile is eating me out of house and home. You ain't full yet?"
"Mama ain't isn't a word."
"I ought to know I was a county school teacher for 20 years. Girls come and scratch my head."


14 months ago

The Slclc held their meeting at the christ temple church. It was a phenomenon to behold. A very intelligent man once said that it is in your highest moment that Satan tests you.
We've read the story of Job and how horrific it became. Some people like to compare their trials in life to that of Job. But how many people wanted to live like Jobs?
"... so It is with our deepest regret that we are departing from this congregation, Reverend Dr. Waters."

" like that? With no real explanation?" "I've explained fully in our resignation letter, best as I could."

"What's the real reason? You and I both know it's deeper than the dress code of the church."

"Maybe you should take a look at the whole church. It's a real circus and a whole lot of commotion."

"A commotion that paid you… we know why, it should have been you giving your sermon at a conference? You are shaking Dr. King's hand."
He looked at the associate minister silent but deadly.
"We are leaving and it's nothing personal but I prayed about it and we talked. We feel it's best to go now."

"But it's personal for me. We've lost 150 members, all who shared the same exact sentiment."

"Maybe it's a coincidence that this happened. Or maybe it's not up to us to decide where the Lord's sheep decide to go." The associate minister remained smug.
"Just come clean and say you wanted to preach more and you wanted more time and exposure with all that is going on. But don't tell me you're leaving and it's not personal. Because it's personal to me and costs me something." David balled his muddy colored fist up and slammed it on the desk in his pastoral office.

" Thirty years, thirty, this church has been open. And for 25 you've been the associate minister."

Silence filled the room up until the very moment that Lady Waters stepped in. Though she was known for being poised and graceful, she was also a tough cookie. And stood by her husband and the ministry by any means necessary.
"Gentlemen? Am I interrupting something?"
"Evidently, Ethel, can't you see us having an important conversation." the minster boldly replied.
"Behind these 4 walls it's Lady Ethel. Minister vixen. But I can do you one better, we release you from this auspice and we accept your resignation letter. For whatever particular reason it may be a reasonable justification or not. However you will not sit here and disrespect my husband, our leader. And you don't get to be rude in the house of the Lord."
" and a woman should know her place in the house of the Lord." in an irritable manner, the minister stands up and grabs his belongings.

"I've held my tongue long enough, I've served this church and the community for years and I've been preaching long before you established this here." he pointed around the room.

" Everyone can talk about how great you and your family are, but I know the real you. The one who had to borrow my car to pick up Ethel for courting sessions. The one who lived in a 1 bedroom apartment with kids growing up, the one where your wife couldn't get a teaching job til I put in a good word for her." as the minister ranted. David sat back in his chair to listen. Removing his glasses, he used the edge of his dress shirt to clear up the fog on them, after he placed them back on his face.
"Are you finished?"he cleared his voice.
"We are thankful for your time and contributions, but I fear if you don't leave this office now, our brethren won't be so patient."
David's adjutants stood on each side of the door, waiting to aid him at any inconvenience.

"Good bye, may God have mercy on your soul." the minister coldly replied before kicking the door open and departing from the church.


Christmas week was finally upon them, David Sr. was starting to miss his family. Not that he never missed them, but he was a busy man, a man of the cloth. Called at every opportunity and hour of the day. Which at times could be exhausting. His family understood him, especially Ethel who was his safe haven. This holiday season would be a wonderful gift to him, seeing he had been sick and under pressure.

When David Jr arrived, he wanted to speak to Ethel first. Tensions weren't great when he told his dad he was leaving the church to go to Detroit and join the Motown record company. David Jr had played for the world's greatest artist, and composed some good records. His Dad could be proud of that, maybe not so much snorting powder cocaine, or drinking and smoking marijuana.

In Spite of his vices, he wasn't what he did. And it was something about being back home that could renew your meaning of self.

When he walked into the door and his feet hit the pavement of the kitchen floor, Ethel jumped from the sudden noise. She was making plates of food for her husband. David noticed his mother sporting two pigtails down her back, a blouse, cardigan, and pleated slacks. He could not believe his eyes. It seems like she was progressing with the times.
"Mama!" David Jr. yelled excitedly. Ethel's eyes had lit up seeing her baby boy.
"Baby boy, how are you?" she said. She grabbed her son, hugging him mercilessly. David Jr. towered over her, hugging back.

It had been almost a year since he saw her, he wrote to her and called as often as he could.
"You look so different!." she commented. Soon after someone rang the doorbell.
"Get that for me, will you? I have to take this plate to your daddy." he obliged and grabbed the door. It turned out that it was Julius who had just come from the barbershop.
"Uncle Julius, my man."

"Cat daddy, give me some love." Julius replied. They did their secret handshake and lastly hugged.
He came in and took his coat off. North Carolina weather was unpredictable , it was winter but it could be sunny one minute and snowing the next.
"Man it's Freezing out there, I know David and Ethel would have us toasty here." he joked rubbing his hands together. He detected the smell of Fried chicken, sweet potato pie and greens steaming in the pot. David Jr. knew he would have to face his father either way.
" DJ, you okay? You look a little worried."

"Yes I'm good." Julius wasn't convinced by his nephew's answer so he prodded more out of him.
"Are you really?"

"Dad wants me to be here and become music minister, I haven't lived life yet. It's too much pressure. I can't be the perfect man he wants me to be. Uncle Julius I've messed up, really bad. I was scared the night Stephen got killed. And like a punk I ran away."

"Did he ever say he wanted you to be perfect?" Julius asks.
"Not with his mouth, but his actions." David Jr. explained.

"Maybe talking to him again will help, but you are a man, and you make the best decisions for yourself. I'm not gonna be the one to tell you that you shouldn't be a music minister, but I won't tell you that you shouldn't. Come on"
Julius twisted the door handle of the master bedroom and welcomed his nephew.

Coughing and holding a glass of water, the reverend looked up. Ethel wrapped up his plate in aluminum foil and velma and Heidi sat around his bedside.

"Son." He said solemnly.

It would have been warranted if David Sr. would have been berating his son, for going missing and choosing a different path than he expected. Going completely cross the line that him and his mother drew for the kids. But David Sr. is reminded of the scripture that says, train up a child in the way they should go and when they are older they won't depart from it. Ethel and David did their level best to teach the kids right from wrong, and to have their own personal relationship with God. They wanted to blame themselves for the questionable decisions their children made but it wouldn't have made sense.

'Foolishness is in the heart of a child.' he once quoted in one of his sermons. The only difference was that even though they were his children, in society they were full grown adults.

Instead of doing what was expected from a well known pastor and preacher. He took his spectacle's of judgement off and opted to give a warm embrace to his namesake.

Relieved, DJ squeezed him tighter, but he didn't want to do it too much because he didn't know how frail his father was.
"Welcome home, you going to go out tonight in town with your buddies or you staying for dinner?"

"Dad I'm home, I'm staying for some of mom's good cooking. And spend time with my old man if that's permitted." he chuckled slightly.
"Always son, always." David Sr. grins.
Hearing noise and combustion they turned their heads slightly ajar to the door that was opening. Velma and a gentleman that DJ hadn't been acquainted with, walked in.
The reverend sat up some more, Ethel came and fixed his pillow.
"Minister Evers, such a wonderful surprise to see you today."

He took his hat off and walked across the room to shake David Sr. hand.
"Oh Reverend I had to come see you today, and when Lady Waters invited me for dinner I couldn't pass up the opportunity." he said excitedly. Everyone laughed in the room.
Carter Evers was around 5'8 and had a mid- brown complexion. He wore his minister attire just about everywhere with the white collar enclasped around his neck.

"Son I want you to meet this fine young man, Carter Evers."
"How's it going man?" David said greeting him with a handshake.
Evers stood tall with a warm smile pleasured to make his soon to be brother in- law acquaintance.
"Evers is the new music minister at the church, he's doing excellent work." David Jr.'s father exclaimed.

His smile faltered a little bit. But not to the point where it was super noticeable.
"That's good dad, really good." he replied.
"Not good like you man, I'm just doing whatever I can to serve the Lord." Evers humbly stated.
Ethel stood up from her post and looked over at Velma.
"Velma don't you have anything you want to share with your brother?" she eyed her daughter across the room.

Velma silently assumes her position by Carter's side.
"Oh yes." she clears her throat and smiles politely.
"DJ, Minister Evers and I are engaged to be married." she informed him.
Carter happily grabs velma's hand and kisses it while looking at her in the eyes.
Although Velma seems welcoming and accommodating of it, David being her brother could see that she wasn't exactly comfortable. But as Pastor kids, they were taught to never let their real emotions show in situations, it was impolite and downright not christian of them.
"Well then congratulations are in order sis!" he exclaimed. Once again shaking Carter's hand and hugging his sister.

"We'll talk." he whispered in his sister's ear. Velma nodded in response.
When the reverend could get into a place where he was mobilized then thats when everyone sat together for dinner.

The last couple of years had been detrimental to the family and the ministry. It was just nice to just exhale for a moment and be with family. The kids weren't exactly in ministry anymore. The reverend was even on sabbatical because of his health scare. Ethel ran her tailor shop and helped kept the church going with hiring other ministers to preach on sunday's. Half of the church had left. David Sr. didn't feel he was in a favorable position. What crushed his spirit the most though, was his kids leaving and doing exactly what others from the outside said they would do, backslide.
He rebuked them, he did what any father who was in his position would do.
And that was understandable with the family being a pillar in the community and somewhat of a moral standard. But the stress and the weight of it all got to him. He gave his children over to the Lord, for now he would enjoy the holidays.
Not bring up their indiscretions, their choices, and vices.

One day the Christ of temple church would return back to its glory and excellence that people admired. But for now everyone was home, that's little or insignificant to others. But to the Reverend it meant a great deal. No matter what they struggled with or what they did, he was true to his words that the backsliders, his children were always welcomed home.

## Epilogue

Sister Gracie placed a vase of flowers on David's sr. desk in the pastor's study. With her white gloves, she inspected the dust particles and shined the rest of his office. She was excited about the

pastor coming back from his sabbatical. And so was the rest of the faithful portion of the congregation. Although some people rather attend bedside baptist because they didn't approve of the guest speakers who filled in for him. The office door cracked open, and the pastor glided in the room in his full clerical attire. Right behind him holding his bible and her purse slung over her shoulder, Ethel.
"Reverend! Lady Waters, welcome back." She hugged them tightly.
"Likewise sister Gracie." the Reverend spoke.
They were both very grateful to Gracie for her kindness and servitude. She made it pretty easy for them with the transition taking place. Ethel wanted the reverend to take it easy since he just got back to normal.
Suddenly they heard a thud near the office door. They also heard a few voices murmuring.
"Who's that?" Ethel asked.
Smiling so hard , till her cheeks raised Gracie answered, " it's the carolinian newspaper. They've come to interview you guys. They wanted the whole family but I couldn't promise that. Seeing that your girls and DJ are all doing their own thing."

The Reverend, appeased with the situation, looked at Ethel and wanted to see if she approved.
"Actually the kids are all home for the holiday season, and plus you know Velma's wedding is coming up. This may not be the best time Gracie, with everything going on and the reverend getting back on his feet." she detests looking sternly between the two of them.
"Hear me out First Lady, after sister Jackson's boy funeral, and Vixen leaving the church taking the other members and starting their own church a couple of blocks down the road. Not only that but taking our soloist Lorraine with them, this is the perfect opportunity to bring light to the ministry. The community misses y'all, they may as well call you the black mayor of Beverdille, Reverend." Gracie rants.

"You make a fair point sister," he says. He doesn't make his decision yet because he knows his wife has been worried about him taking it easy. But if looks could talk this seemed like a great opportunity to him. Catching his expression, Ethel perks up.

"Well… how many questions?" Ethel asked
"Just a few First Lady, I promise."
"A few?"
"A few." Gracie smiles.

Lady nodded her head and finally gave her approval. That was when Sister Gracie opened the office door and welcomed the journalist in. A young black gentleman and a young woman entered. The gentleman possessed a camera and his partner , a notepad with a pencil. The interview would begin shortly.

The Church of Christ temple would be front page and center.

Made in the USA
Columbia, SC
05 January 2025

399f6ffe-25f7-46ae-b36e-3bfad6f87fe2R01